Not A Fire Exit

Thank you—

Hillary
Schmidt

Not A
Fire Exit

Christopher M. Finlan

MILVERSTEAD PUBLISHING
Philadelphia | Portland

ISBN-13: 978-0-9842847-0-2
ISBN-10: 0-9842847-0-2

Cover and interior design: Marin Bookworks
Cover photo: Victor Miles Photography
Cover model: Sarah McMaster
Editing: Heather Goodman

This book is a work of fiction. Names, characters, businesses, organizations, places, events and incidents either are the product of the author's
imagination or are used fictitiously. Any resemblance to actual persons,
living or dead, or actual events is entirely coincidental.

Milverstead Publishing
31 Rampart Drive
Chesterbrook, PA 19087
(888) 667-3981

Visit us on the web!
www.notafireexit.com

dedication

To Zane Schmid and the Schmid family, whose passion and dedication as they fight to find a cure for Spinal Muscular Atrophy has inspired so many to accomplish so much.

". . . the greatest defeat of all would be to live without courage, for that would hardly be living at all."
—GERALD FORD

"All my life I've had one dream, to achieve my many goals."
—HOMER SIMPSON

foreword

"There they are," said the ultrasound technician. "What?" I exclaimed. Simultaneously, my mouth opened wide, my body shook, and tears flowed as she informed my husband Keith and I that we would be expecting twins. I was overjoyed, shocked, and scared.

I had a great pregnancy, and we soon learned we were having twin girls. I pictured dressing them the same, braiding their hair, and getting them on the school bus for the first time. So many "firsts" were about to happen.

The girls were born in January 2009. Avery and Zane were beautiful and healthy. We couldn't stop looking at them. Avery looked like Keith, and Zane looked like me. Those days were joyfully tiresome and busy.

I can remember it vividly. On their one month birthday, we took their picture, in matching outfits of course. Keith and I noticed Zane was not moving her head or legs as much as she was previously, but we didn't think much of it. Two weeks later, the girls had a routine pediatrician appointment. I discussed our observations with the doctor. He assessed Zane, made a few phone calls, and suggested that Keith and I immediately take Zane to the emergency room. I was confused and scared. This was supposed to be a "routine" appointment, and now we were going to the emergency room?

After a grueling couple of days of tests, poking and prodding, Zane was diagnosed with Spinal Muscular Atrophy- Type I. We had never heard of this disease. The doctors explained what SMA was, informed us of the type of life a child with SMA leads, and most devastatingly, told us that she may not live past her first birthday. Our daughter had a terminal disease and statistics said she would only live a few more months. How could this be? We were devastated, shocked, confused, and angry.

There were times I found myself sobbing uncontrollably, and I felt like I didn't know how to stop crying. I hated SMA. Keith and I shared many hugs over those next few days with few words spoken between us. We both couldn't believe what had transpired. As we embraced our two girls, their smiles lead to our tears. As we stared at them, then focused on Zane, we shook our heads in disbelief. In the beginning, I would look at Zane and think to myself, "Is today the day we will lose her?"

In what seemed like a surreal moment, I stopped thinking like that. Zane had so many people that loved her. We had excellent medical care, and with our determination to help her fight this disease, she was going to beat SMA. I knew the statistics, but said, "It's not going to be our daughter!" I truly felt she was going to beat this disease. She was special, a gift from God, and we weren't going to give her back without a fight. I sprung into *I am going to do everything* mode to save her.

We were lucky to have Zane healthy for three months. Slowly, she started moving less and less, lost the ability to swallow, and she began to lose the tone in her muscles. All while having a smile on her face. The minds of children with SMA are unaffected. They tend to be very social and intellectual. Zane loved people. When she looked at you, she gave you her undivided attention.

She had big brown eyes with long eyelashes. People were drawn towards her. One of her favorite activities (Keith's too) was when he would lay her on her back and move her legs back and forth rapidly pairing his voice with the movements. She would gaze and smile at him. Avery and Zane were always together: on the play mat, in a crib, in a stroller, or sitting with us on the couch. They explored each other's clothing and faces. Eventually, Zane needed arm slings to manipulate things in front of her. Other times, the girls would just smile at each other, sitting in silence.

Those three months were also a time of pure chaos. Weekly, if not daily doctor's appointments, in home medical training, continuous medical equipment deliveries, early intervention therapies, insurance paperwork, locating and/or making adaptive equipment, countless phone calls, and trying to successfully run a household. We did it with support. Support from each other, our wonderful families, our fantastic friends, the community, and Families of Spinal Muscular Atrophy— www.fsma.org. Whether it was one person or a group, each party in their own way helped our family through this difficult time.

Zane became ill one beautiful spring day in May. She was pale, really pale. Her oxygen levels were low, and she was struggling to breathe. I looked at Keith, and he returned the frightened look back to me. That thought came to me. "Is today THE day?" Frantically, we loaded her into the car and drove to the emergency room. She was admitted for twenty-seven days. Zane had contracted the flu. There were many days of one step forward and three steps backwards. She had to fight, and she did. Some days were harder than others for her. She always smiled except when it was time to put the Bi- Pap mask on her. The hospital staff was caring and comforting. They loved Zane, and she loved them. Between Keith, myself, and our compassionate circle of family and friends, Zane was never alone. There was always someone there to cheer her on. Slowly her condition started to improve. The discussion of being discharged was so exciting. At one point, I was jumping up and down while holding her in my arms. Avery and Zane had not seen each other in twenty-seven days, aside from pictures. We couldn't wait to have our family together again.

I brought Zane home that day. She slept in the car. At every red light, I turned around and looked at her. Sometimes I smiled or shed tears of joy and relief that she was healthy again. When the girls saw each other, Avery reached forward in Zane's direction. Zane looked at Avery, and she started whimpering. Keith and I thought this moment was going to be more than it was. As the hours passed, we noticed Zane sounded congested. We had to suction her frequently. I was getting nervous, but didn't voice my feelings out loud.

Within twelve hours of being home, we called 911. It was 2 a.m. Zane's breathing was shallow; she was pale, and barely responsive. Before the ambulance arrived, Keith and I talked to her, provided oxygen, and quickly repacked to go back to the hospital. We were running on adrenalin.

The hospital staff couldn't believe we were back and so quickly. Zane's smile was absent and she seemed listless. It felt different this time; she was different. I did not leave her side for three days. On the third day, the doctors approached Keith and me. As we sat in the small room, weeping, they presented Zane's options to us. Although I was making eye contact and trying to listen, I just kept thinking, "How am I here right now having this discussion?" Keith sat next to me while holding my hand. I couldn't look at him without falling apart. Zane's condition was deteriorating. With all possible medical procedures being done, Zane was suffering. As we looked into her sullen eyes, we felt she was telling us she couldn't fight anymore and that it would be alright. Nature took its course. Keith and I lay in bed with her, embracing her for two hours as she peacefully passed away. Our beautiful, five-month-old daughter rested in our arms. She was at peace; she was free of a debilitating disease. This is Spinal Muscular Atrophy.

Since Zane's passing, Keith and I have grieved together and alone, similarly and differently. When Avery sees Zane's picture, she reaches for it. She smiles at her twin. Although she will have no memory of Zane, we will share our memories and tell her how brave her twin sister fought this disease.

For weeks, I was in shock, disbelief. I seemed to function at times as if there was nothing wrong. I would cry, but then I found myself in Zane's room putting away her clothes. I have come to terms with Zane's death. Throwing myself into raising awareness for SMA, helping to fundraise, and talking to anyone who will listen is how I am coping with my daughter's death. We will continue our quest until there is a cure for SMA. The fact that there is promising stem cell research being done gives us great hope that children may be cured. Yes, we wish it was Zane, but it is not. God had a different purpose for her. Zane's story has inspired so many people; friends, family members, acquaintances, and strangers across the country. This book is an example of one person being inspired by a five-month-old baby.

Chris was inspired by Zane. We want to thank him for writing this story. It will teach you a bit about SMA and what a child and family experiences. It touched our hearts that he wanted to write this book even though he never met Zane. So, Chris, thank you for your hard work, time, and vision in creating this superb story.

Hillary Dunlop Schmid

prologue

Beth Groves glanced at the small clock as it chimed 10:00 p.m. It was one of the few things she'd brought this humid July night before they'd rushed to University of Philadelphia hospital from her father's home in Wynnewood, twenty minutes from center city Philadelphia. She had never heard of Type One Spinal Muscular Atrophy when she gave birth to Michele on Valentine's Day five months ago. Now, she'd read more on the subject than she'd ever dreamed, and it all told her the same thing. Her daughter was going to die.

She kissed and rubbed her daughter's pale forehead as she sat by Michele's bedside, trying not to disturb the ugly BiPap breathing apparatus that covered her daughter's face. It was the machine she hated the most because her daughter's smile disappeared each time she'd have to wear it. Her smile had been the last thing Beth had to keep her going as Michele's body shut down from the disease, and now it was gone too.

"Please God," Beth said, listening to the heart monitor's rhythmic beep as she prayed. "Please make this terrible disease go away."

The door swung open as Beth's father entered. He placed his jacket on the table and walked over to her. "How is she, sweetheart?"

Beth looked up at him and shook her head as she continued to stroke her daughter's hair and face. "I'm losing her, Daddy," she said, "I just wish Steve—"

"I know, Beth. I know."

Beth's dad placed his large hands on Beth's shoulders and leaned over and kissed his granddaughter. Beth buried her head into her father's chest as he embraced her.

"Is Melissa here yet?" she asked, her voice muffled as she spoke into his gray turtleneck.

"She's on her way." The room phone rang, and he said, "That must be her. You answer it and tell her I'm coming downstairs to sign her in." Her father kissed the top of her head as he headed for the door. Getting visitors up to the room was a frustrating exercise since it required one of them to leave Michele for up to ten minutes just to retrieve anyone.

He headed out of the room as she picked up the phone on the third ring.

"Hey sis, Dad will be right down," she said.

"Excuse me?" the unfamiliar voice asked.

"Oh, I'm sorry," she said. "I thought it was my sister arriving."

"Ah, I see," he said. "No Mrs. Groves, my name is Dr. Thomas Schad, and I'm calling to speak to you about your daughter. Her name is Michele, correct?"

"Well, yes, but—"

"And she has Type One Spinal Muscular Atrophy?"

"Who is this again?" she asked.

"Like I said Mrs. Groves, my name is Dr. Schad. Dr. Thomas Schad."

"Have we met before, Dr. Schad?"

"No, Mrs. Groves, we haven't. I was only recently contacted by someone who felt I could help Michele."

She tried to think who could have called him, maybe the hospital administrator, a doctor on call, or a nurse.

"I'm not quite sure I understand, doctor," she said. "I've seen or talked to just about every SMA specialist in the country, and I've never heard your name mentioned during our conversations."

"Well, I don't specialize in SMA. I'm more of a 'jack of all trades'."

"Look, I'm sorry, Dr. Schad, I don't know who contacted you, but my father and I—"

"Beth, I can cure your daughter."

She covered her mouth. "But, but how. They said—"

"They're wrong. I promise you."

She didn't respond. Instead she glanced at her daughter's breathing apparatus.

"Mrs. Groves, we need to continue the rest of this conversation in person if you're interested in what I have to say. There's a small office just a short walk from the hospital."

"Well, yes, of course I'm interested. But my daughter—I'm afraid to leave her side in case something happens. I'd really prefer to do the meeting here."

"I understand your reluctance to leave her, Mrs. Groves, but everything has already been set up at the office. Perhaps your father could remain with Michele while we go over the details here."

The doctor on-call had assured her Michele would sleep for the next few hours because of the intravenous pain medication she was receiving. However, Michele's condition was grave, and leaving her daughter's side, even for a moment, seemed crazy to her. But if there was any hope, any chance that what this guy said was true, didn't she owe it to Michele to at least check it out?

"How did you know my father—"

"Everything will be explained once you arrive," he said. "The address is 1425 Spruce Street, Office 4B. It's just up the elevator to the second floor and down the hall on your right. I'll make sure the lobby doors are unlocked by the time you get here at say, 10:30? That should give you plenty of time."

She glanced at the clock—it was 10:10 p.m.

"Don't worry, Mrs. Groves, everything is going to be just fine."

With that, the line went dead. She set the phone down and stood for a moment, staring at her daughter.

Her father opened the door, cleaning the lid of a Diet Sprite as he attempted to close the door behind him with his leg.

"Your sister wasn't there," he said. "Figured I wouldn't waste the trip and got you something to drink. Here you go."

He pushed the soda towards her, but she didn't move or take her eyes off Michele.

"Beth? What is it?"

"Some guy named Dr. Schad just called," she said.

"Dr. Schad? Who's Dr. Schad?"

"I, I'm not sure . . ."

"Here, tell me what happened."

Her father pulled the other chair over in front of Michele's bed and faced her. He opened the soda can and handed it to her again. She took a long sip before she returned it to him.

"Okay, so what exactly did this guy say?"

"He said his name was Dr. Thomas Schad, and he's some sort of specialist who can cure Michele."

"Cure her? Oh, c'mon."

"Yes, he claimed he could cure her. He wants me to meet him at some office just down the street while you stay with Michele."

"Absolutely not," her father said, standing up from his chair and waving her off as he walked over to the window. "He's obviously a fraud."

"But Dad—"

"No, I'm not letting my daughter go off in the middle of the night to speak with some snake oil salesman who's preying on her emotions."

She walked over to her father and looked out the window with him.

"What would Mom have done?"

He half-chuckled and looked down. "She'd already have told me to stuff it and be out the door."

"I was praying for a miracle, Daddy," she said. "Maybe this Dr. Schad is the answer to my prayers."

"But he's not, Beth," he said, shaking his head. "I see people like this all the time—"

She fought back tears and placed her head on her father's chest. "Please, Daddy. I don't care. I have to try."

He wrapped his arms around her, and he stroked her hair. "Beth, you know I'd do anything for you and Michele, but—"

She sighed, remembering when her father used to hold her, whether it was when she'd had a fever or gotten scared by a thunderstorm. "What if it was me, Daddy?" she asked. "What would you do if it was me?"

He rubbed his daughter's back. "I'd do anything, sweetheart. You know that."

She wiped her eyes as she pulled back from him. "Then you know I have to do this for Michele," she said.

"Alright, sweetheart, alright," he said. "But at least let me go and see what his story is."

"No, Daddy," she said. "I'm her mother. It's my job, not yours, and I'm going."

She grabbed her purse and checked her appearance in the mirror on the door. He brushed the lint from the sleeve of her shirt.

"Be careful, Beth," he said. "You call me the minute you're done."

"I will," she said. "I love you, Dad."

"I love you, too." They embraced for a moment before she walked to Michele's bedside. The breathing machine hummed in her ear as she leaned over to kiss her daughter's tiny hand, which Michele couldn't move on her own any longer. She kissed and cradled it in her own.

"I won't let you down, sweetie," she whispered. "I promise." She squeezed Michele's hand and headed out the door.

Beth arrived at 1425 Spruce Street just fifteen minutes after she'd hung up with Dr. Schad. The building was a non-descript office complex, one of a dozen similar structures that dotted the area around the sprawling hospital grounds. She'd passed it before when they'd had to park in the adjacent private lot during her daughter's previous visits. The white building numerals above the outer doors had faded, and few lights in the lobby were on. Taking a deep breath, she headed towards the front entrance.

She pushed open the lobby door and hurried inside. The small lobby wasn't decorated, and an inactive fountain covered most of it, flanked by a pair of benches that formed a virtual "V". She walked across the empty lobby to the bank of elevators, unnerved by the sound of the occasional drip of water from the fountain head splashing into the murky blue pool below.

She stepped out of the elevator as the doors opened to the second floor. Unlike the lobby, there were no lights on in the hallway at all; the only light came from the open doorway on the right side of the hall. No nameplate hung noting the room number or Dr. Schad. She peered inside the office and saw an older man sitting at a single desk in the middle of the room working on a laptop. The desk also had a phone, small printer and green lamp on it that provided the light for the room. Another door was to the left of the desk, with a sign on it that said 'Warning— Not A Fire Exit'. There was a single folding chair on her side of the desk.

"Hello? Dr. Schad?" she asked as she knocked on the open door.

He lifted his head and looked her over before returning to his work. "Please have a seat, Mrs. Groves," he said as he directed her to the open chair. "I'll be with you momentarily." He was white and in his late fifties, his hair and thick beard and moustache mostly white, save for some flecks of black. His vintage grey pinstripe suit was buttoned and tailored, and his thin-rimmed glasses pressed against his nose and face.

She unzipped her jacket and tucked her long skirt under her as she sat down on the uncomfortable metal chair. Dr. Schad ignored her presence as he tapped away on the keyboard for another minute before the printer came to life and spit out multiple sheets of paper. He drummed his hand on the desk and glanced at his watch while she shifted in her seat as the machine droned on.

"I apologize for the delay. I know you must be eager to get started," he said. The printer stopped, and he flipped through the stack of papers for a few moments. He nodded and placed the papers on the desk facing her.

"There we go," he said. "Shall we begin, Mrs. Groves?"

She nodded and pulled her chair up. "Please, call me Beth," she said.

"Very well, Beth, as I told you during our phone call, my name is Dr. Thomas Schad. Here's my card."

He handed her a faded business card that almost slipped through her fingers as she took it from him. It simply read—

Dr. Thomas Schad
(888) 667-3981

"I'm not a specialist in this area," he said, "but this particular treatment has proven to be effective with a wide variety of patients and their various diseases, including Michele's. However, I'd like to review her official records online before I get into specifics about the procedure. Would that be okay with you?"

"Yes, please, whatever you need," she said.

"Alright, I'll just need you to sign at the bottom of the top page where I've indicated with an X." Dr. Schad took a gold pen from his coat pocket and handed it to her. She scribbled her signature in the bottom box and handed the page to him. "Don't you even want to read it?" he asked.

"I've read that same HIPAA form a hundred times," she said. "I could recite it by heart."

"I know," he said. "But I want you to trust me about everything I have you sign. Here, just take a moment and make sure you're comfortable with it." He handed the paper back to her, and she read the generic HIPAA release form giving him access to Michele's records.

"This is fine," she said and slid it back to him. "I appreciate the thought, though."

He nodded and placed the paper in an empty manila folder he pulled out of the desk drawer and typed in some information on his laptop. He lifted his glasses and squinted at the output on the screen and returned to the paper to jot down some notes. It took about three minutes to finish writing down everything he needed off the screen. *What is taking so long*, she thought, checking her cell phone and sighing when she saw the "No Service" message on her phone.

"Well this is good news," he said. "It appears I can have your daughter completely cured and fully recovered within three days."

"Three days?" she asked, pushing the hair out of her face. "That's, that's not possible."

"Of course it is," he said. "Here, take a look for yourself." He spun the laptop screen towards her and enlarged the window with Michele's information. There were several complex mathematical equations on the screen and her vital statistics. Directly above this information spun a 3-D image of Michele, including the birthmark on the back of her right thigh. Blinking in the bottom right hand corner was the following information: "Predicted Death Rate—Zero percent. Prognosis—Full Recovery."

She tapped her teeth with her thumbnail as she stared at the information. "This is certainly impressive," she said. "But I'm not—"

"Convinced?" he asked. "I wouldn't expect you to be. It's only a computer simulation, after all, and I know how every doctor Michele's seen has been telling you that your daughter's condition is both incurable and fatal. But I wouldn't have pulled you away from her side if I couldn't do exactly what I just told you."

Beth rubbed her earlobe as he spoke.

"I'm sorry, Dr. Schad," she said, shaking her head. "I want to believe you, I really do, it's just—"

"Part of you thinks I'm nuts, right?" he asked as he leaned closer and smirked.

"Well . . ." she said, looking at the floor.

He chuckled. "Alright, maybe all of you think I'm nuts. That's okay, you're not the first, and you certainly won't be the last. But I'm not about to lie to you in any way. It would not only be a breach of our contract, but I'd be costing myself a considerable amount of money, since with this procedure I don't get paid unless the treatment is successful."

"I'd pay any price to save Michele," she said.

"Of course, Beth," he said. "That's why I'm here. So let's get down to business."

Dr. Schad got up from his chair and came around the desk. He smiled as he walked past her and looked in the hallway before continuing. She read through the remaining paperwork as he settled back into his chair.

He said, "So, what we need to do—"

She put up her hand to cut him off. "What's this part here about some person called the host?" she asked as she pointed at the paperwork.

"That section refers to the obligations of the two involved parties besides me, who are identified in the contract as the patient and the host," he said.

"Who is the host?"

"That's what I wanted to explain. Before you commit to anything, it's important I go over the details of the procedure and the financial options you'll have. This information is also covered in the documents in front of you, and you're under no obligation to do anything until you sign. But this agreement cannot be changed, altered, or re-structured for any reason. You either accept all the terms and conditions or you don't. Do you understand?"

The room was silent as he waited for her response. She nodded and set the paperwork back down in front of her.

"Very well," he said. "This procedure is straightforward, but it's more complicated for certain children under the age of one. The host has to meet certain criteria and that can vary greatly based on the patient's age and vital statistics."

"Alright . . ?" she said.

"So, getting back to your question, the host is someone who is the approximate age, sex, ethnic background, and weight of the patient. It's also very important the new host is free from any sort of major medical issues of his or her own, things like deformities, birth defects, etc. What I always tell people is the host basically can't have anything that can't be treated at one of those drugstore clinics. That's the easiest way to think of it. Hosts are carefully screened before the procedure begins anyway, but letting people know that upfront saves a lot of time and aggravation later on."

"I'm sorry, I'm not sure I'm following you. Are you saying another little girl needs to be a part of this procedure?"

He nodded and opened the bottom desk drawer, removing a bottle of water and two plastic cups. He set the two cups on the desk in front of her, pouring part of the bottle into the cup on the left.

"I used to try and just explain this part," he said. "But I've found it's easier for people to follow if I use these props. Now, this cup with the water is Michele, and this other cup is the host I've been speaking of."

Taking an Alka-Seltzer packet from his coat pocket, he ripped open the package and dropped the tablets into the Michele cup. "The chemical compound I've developed is injected into Michele's body, causing a similar reaction with her SMA to what you see happening with the water in this cup," he said. "As you can see, this reaction is immediate and rather violent, and needs to be out of her system as quickly as possible. So it's moved." He poured the fizzing water into the empty cup. "To the host, thus leaving Michele free of both her disease and the chemicals I've used. A day or two of bed rest, and she'll be as good as new."

"But, but what about this cup?" Beth asked as she pointed at it on the desk. "What happens to the other little girl, the host?"

Dr. Schad dropped his head and took a long breath. He wiped his nose and replaced his glasses before he continued. "The host dies, Beth," he explained. "There's simply no other way the procedure will work."

"You can't mean . . ." She avoided his eyes as the impact of what he'd said sunk in. Her face turned white and she sat in stunned silence for several moments before she covered her mouth.

"Here, please, have something to drink," he said as he slid the half-empty water bottle across the desk to her.

She ignored the offer and shook her head. "How could you?" she asked.

"How could I what?" he asked. "All I did was explain how the procedure worked."

"You said you've done this with children before!"

"Well I have, but—"

The chair almost tipped over as she bolted up out of it. "Then you're a monster. An inhuman monster who murders children for your own profit!"

"I resent that!" he said. "I'm a doctor who—"

She waved him off and swung her purse over her shoulder. "You're no doctor," she said. "You're the devil."

Dr. Schad searched his pockets and pulled out a crumpled Post-It note. "On the contrary, Mrs. Groves," he said, grabbing the phone off his desk and dialing. "I'll think you'll find I'm the answer to your prayers."

He paused for a moment as he held the phone to his ear. "Go ahead," he said and slammed the phone down, glaring at her as she gathered her coat.

"I'd like to show you something before you storm out of here." He whipped the laptop around towards her and hit the enter key to bring up a new web browser. Nothing happened on the screen. He held up one finger as she moved towards the door.

"I've got nothing more to—" She froze as the video of Michele came up on the computer screen. The camera must have been directly over her daughter's bed at the hospital. Michele was awake. Her blue eyes looked into the camera.

"Michele," Beth whispered. She retook her seat and pulled the laptop closer. Dr. Schad walked around the desk and folded his arms as he stood beside her. Without warning, Michele's back arched and her mouth opened wide. Since there was no sound, it was impossible to tell if she was screaming or simply gasping for breath.

"Oh god, what did you do to her?" she asked.

"Give it a moment," he said.

Michele was joined in frame by Beth's father and then a nurse, who was attempting to adjust some of the attached machines that were wrenched loose by her daughter's sudden movement. They pushed on Michele's chest to bring her back to the bed. Her head turned from side to side as they held her down and then, nothing. There was no movement of any kind as her eyes closed.

"You killed her!" Beth screamed as she jumped up and lunged towards him. He grabbed her hands as she attempted to strike him and turned her back towards the monitor.

"Mrs. Groves, please, just watch the screen!" he said as he struggled to control her.

As she tried to break free from Dr. Schad's grip, the video feed showed Michele's eyes open. She smiled. Her arms and legs, which hadn't moved in weeks, now kicked and swung without restriction. She turned her head and continued to kick about as she saw her grandfather, who kissed and hugged her while she grabbed at his nose and fingers. The nurse scurried off camera and brought the doctor back with her to examine Michele.

As Beth watched, she stopped fighting Dr. Schad and now embraced him. To his shoulder she kept saying, "Thank you, thank you."

"I'm very happy you're pleased with these results, but I must caution you," he said as he pulled her away and looked her in the eyes, "this was only a temporary solution to stabilize her for the full treatment. Without a signed agreement in place in the next two hours, this will wear off, and she'll be back on life support and die shortly thereafter, just as she would have if I hadn't intervened."

Beth turned back towards the screen, which showed her daughter with more spirit and energy than at any other time in her short life. She bowed her head towards the floor and pulled at her left arm with her right hand.

"I, I just don't think I can just grab someone's child and—"

"You're not grabbing anyone," he said. "I told you children this young are more complicated and that's because unlike adults or even older children, they're too young to consent to this procedure on their own. For children under the age of one to be used as a host, a child's biological parent must give their consent. Siblings and children who have been adopted or orphaned are not eligible, and a DNA test is done to verify the identity."

"A parent has to consent?"

He nodded.

"What sort of person would ever agree to such a thing?" she asked.

"Not everyone is as loving and devoted as you are, Mrs. Groves," he said. "I've seen all types of parents in the world, raising their children any number of ways. Why do people give their children up for adoption? Or beat them? Or sell them? Parents are tested by their children every day, and sadly many of them fail to do what's best. I wish every parent was like you, Beth, but I'd be naïve if I believed that would happen."

She sat back in her chair and looked at the floor. She fiddled with her earlobe, looking once again at Dr. Schad.

"And you've seen people agree to this before?" she asked.

"In Michele's case, it isn't an issue. A host has already been identified and the paperwork drawn up."

"It has?"

"That's correct," he said.

"Well who is it?"

"I can't reveal that until you've signed the agreement, but rest assured, the baby doesn't have a parent like you." He looked at his watch and gathered the paperwork, placing it in the manila folder. "I don't mean to rush you, Beth. But I'm sure your father has been trying to contact you about the happy news with Michele, and the cell reception in this building is awful. You have a couple hours to make up your mind, and I want to you to enjoy this time with your daughter and make the right decision."

She nodded and took the folder from him. Michele's face was still visible on the computer screen, and Beth watched every gesture with a growing smile that disappeared when she looked back at the cup of milky water on the desk.

"Is this even legal?" she asked as she rose from her chair.

"That's all covered in the paperwork," he said. "While it's crafted to protect all parties, you shouldn't be concerned with breaking the law. You just worry about the cost of the procedure and doing what's best for your daughter."

"Of course, doctor." She took her purse and pointed at the closed door in the room. "Can I get out that way?"

He glanced over at the warning sign and pointed at the door she used when she arrived. "You can," he said, "But you'd be better off going back the way you came."

"Alright," she said, and headed back towards the hallway. "Goodbye, Dr. Schad. I'll call you soon with my decision."

"Goodbye, Beth," he said. "I'm sure you'll do the right thing for Michele."

She headed back to the elevator, and attempted to dial Michele's room, but the call wouldn't go through until she exited the building. A lone car startled her as it streaked past on the quiet street, and she dropped the phone and folder of information. Picking up the scattered pages, she saw phrases like "chemical burning" and "carcass disposal". Her phone beeped at her feet. It read—

You have 3 Missed Calls.

You have 1 Voicemail.

She picked up the phone to dial her voicemail and pressed the phone to her ear as she dashed across the street.

"Press One to hear new messages, Press—"

Hurry up, she thought, quickly bypassing the rest of the menu. The message began, her face turning ashen as she listened. She stopped and replayed the message from the beginning, hand trembling as she pushed each key. But there was no mistaking Dr. Schad's voice in the message she heard. It consisted of just two words—

"Go ahead."

1

Three months later

"Another damn upward dog? What's next, Sarah, waterboarding?" Jim asked.

The workout DVD had just started, and Sarah Knox was already tired of her husband's incessant whining. He'd promised her that they'd start working out together every morning at the beginning of October, but he had found one excuse after another not to do so. Now that she'd finally forced him to follow through on the promise at 7:30 a.m. on Saturday, he'd done nothing but complain from the moment she pulled him out of bed.

"Yes Jim, I'm sure most terrorists are subject to basic yoga moves to make them talk," she said. "We only have to do this part for two minutes, you big baby."

"Easy for you to say, girls are supposed to be good at stuff like this."

"You realize the instructor's a guy, don't you?"

"He's the exception that proves the rule?"

"Nice try," she said.

"Maybe they're using CGI?" he asked.

"For an exercise video?"

Jim collapsed on the floor, losing his balance again. "Is there any answer here that gets me out of this?"

"No."

"Then sure, what the hell."

Sarah pulled him to his feet and gave him a quick kiss on the cheek as they started the next section. "Try to keep up," she said, smiling as they began jogging in place.

"You know," he said, gasping for breath like he'd been at it four hours instead of four minutes, "I would have been happy to just go biking again."

"Oh really?" she asked. She nodded at a picture of him on the mantle above the fireplace with full cycling gear on, standing next to an expensive looking bike.

"C'mon, that was over three years ago and was an accident."

"You smashed it in the garage with your softball bat!"

"I was off my meds."

"Flintstone Vitamins don't count as meds."

"I respectfully disagree."

"Fine," she said and smoothly transitioned into the next exercise. "Can you cite any other incidents of Flintstone Vitamins causing their users to lash out violently against a birthday present from their wife?"

"I believe some government studies are ongoing."

"Really? Which government would that be? Bedrock's?"

Her question went unanswered as the speaker on Jim's work phone crackled to life in the kitchen.

"Hey, Knox, you there?" asked the voice on Jim's push-to-talk phone.

Jim knocked Sarah from her mat and into the couch as he scrambled to the kitchen counter and grabbed it. The gravelly voice was Jim's supervisor, Derek Sands. He'd been Jim's supervisor at CRC Cable ever since he'd hired Jim as an installer over a year ago, and from what she'd observed from their few short exchanges, beneath Derek's gruff exterior lay yet another gruff exterior.

"Yeah, Derek, hey I'm here," he said. "What's up?"

"That jackass Damon called out sick again. Can you take his service appointments this morning?" Derek asked. "He's only got two, and then Zulowhatever his name is coming on."

Jim glanced over at Sarah, who paused the workout and dabbed at beads of sweat on her face with a towel. She shook her head and mouthed, "No."

"Hey, yeah, sure no problem," he said and ducked to avoid the towel flying by. "What time?"

"Not till 9:30, but I need you to stop at dispatch and get the work orders for each around nine."

"Alright, no problem," he said. "I'll be there."

"Yeah, fine," Derek said. "But don't think this means I owe you one."

Jim set the phone down and snapped his fingers in mock disappointment. "Sorry, Sarah. But you heard Derek," he said. "Duty calls."

"Nice try, honeybunch, but there's no way you're getting out of this that easily. I'll just save this till tonight."

She clicked off the DVD player and flipped to the beginning of the *TODAY* show being recorded with their Tivo. She tossed the remote onto the couch, walked into the kitchen and grabbed a water bottle from the fridge. He shambled over and tried to kiss her, but she pushed him aside as she went back to the family room.

"What are you so mad about?" he asked. "Don't you have that stupid bake sale today anyway?"

"That's not the point, Jim," she said. "We were supposed to work out together today, and you promised me you'd go to the store as well. I'd really, really like you to get to that soon, please."

"Yeah, I saw the color-coded and categorized list you put together. I'll do it later."

"That's what you said yesterday. And the day before that."

"Well I didn't know I was going to have to go into work."

"Oh, I know," she said. "You just had to go in."

"Hey, if you want me around on weekends, I can always take that job in Texas," he said, settling into the recliner in front of the TV. Jim's brother Cam had a sales position open at his company in Austin, but it would mean living down there during the week and flying home to Pennsylvania each weekend. "I have to give him an answer by Friday about that."

"The answer is still no," she said, frowning at the mere mention of the word Texas. "We already decided you're not taking that job."

"Well as long as WE'VE decided," he said. "I think it merits further discussion."

"You really want to be an account executive who sells sporting goods to stores in Texas?"

"Maybe," he said. "Don't forget, my territory would include the entire southwest region. Besides, I'd be making twice the money for half the work."

"Except I'd never get to see you," she said, folding her arms. "I hate it when you bring this up. You know it upsets me."

"Bring what up?" he asked. "The fact that I want to make more money? Or that I want to get back into sales?"

"We don't need the money. We're doing just fine. Just stop talking about it, okay?" she asked.

"Yeah, because we could never use more money. I still want—" He stopped when he saw a commercial for Nolan Realty appear on screen.

"Oh, yes!" he said. "Let's see what Cal's got cooked up for this one." Jim was a huge fan of Cal Nolan, the owner of Nolan Realty who'd inherited the company from his father eighteen months ago. Cal gave Nolan Realty a sexy new image when he took over and fired every realtor the company had and began a nationwide recruiting effort for the "hottest" realtors in the country to come to Philadelphia. He offered a starting base salary of $75,000 plus a tiny commission, which was unheard of in an industry where realtors depended on commission almost exclusively. There was a lot of snickering and outrage about "Hooters Realty," but it worked and was now one of the most successful companies in the Philadelphia area. Much of the company s newfound success was attributed to the accompanying risqué commercials that bordered on soft core porn.

Sarah grabbed the remote and fast-forwarded quickly through the commercial.

"Oh, c'mon," he said. "I wanted to see if that was a new one with Nolan's Knockouts."

"Nolan's Knockouts?"

"Yeah, that's what he's calling them now. This one ad I just saw starts off with this shot of a forest and then—"

"I don't want to know," she said. "Those commercials are all the same anyway. Cal always wears that same cheesy tuxedo while a bunch of his realtors—"

"Knockouts," he corrected her.

"Whatever. I didn't record this show to watch him or his Knockouts in some smutty commercial. I recorded it to watch this." She pointed at the screen and stopped fast-forwarding as a video montage began of a baby girl.

"Coming up next on *TODAY*, we check in on Michele Groves, the remarkable little girl who just three months ago appeared to be hours from death with what's known as SMA, or Spinal Muscular Atrophy, a rare genetic disorder in children. Her sudden and complete recovery from this previously thought to be incurable disease stunned doctors and provided inspiration to millions of Americans. After months of silence, Michele and her mother

Beth are back for another exclusive interview here on the *TO-DAY* show, live, in studio, right after this."

The camera cut to show both mother and daughter sitting on the couch, mom smiling nervously into the camera with her daughter happily playing beside her. The screen faded into another commercial for Nolan Realty. Sarah sighed and hit fast-forward on the remote.

"Wait—who was that again?" he asked. "She looks awfully familiar."

"I already told you, I'm not watching—"

"Not the commercial," he said as he took the remote and rewound to the shot of the mother and daughter. "Her."

Sarah turned and gave him a funny look. "You're kidding, right? That's that little girl I was watching all those stories about a while back."

Jim stared at her blankly.

"Terminal illness suddenly cured? Brings joy to millions? Lives in the area? Any of this ring a bell?"

"I guess," he said. "I remember you crying about some kid on TV. I meant her mom. What was her name?"

"Beth."

"Beth what?"

"Beth Groves, but her maiden name is Snyder. She's been a widow for over a year now, and I read somewhere she might change it, but she apparently never did."

"So she only does interviews for the *TODAY* show or something?"

"Yeah, pretty much. She's had book offers, movie offers, a reality show, you name it, and she's been offered it. So far Beth turned everything down except these two interviews, and she supposedly only agreed to do these as a favor for her sister Melissa who's a producer at the NBC station in town."

Jim snapped his fingers at the screen. "Melissa Snyder!" he shouted. "Yes! That's how I know who that is. Melissa Snyder was two years above me in high school. She had a younger sister Beth who went to an all-girls school, so she could ride horses or something."

"Ride horses?"

"I dunno, something like that. Melissa was the one I cared about. Now there was a girl who would've been perfect as one of Nolan's Knockouts."

"Did you date her or something?"

"Well, if by date you mean masturbated to her picture in '*Teen Magazine* about a thousand times then sure, I dated her."

"OK, first of all—gross," she said. "Second, '*Teen Magazine*? Really?"

"What, I was fifteen. I liked looking at girls my own age."

Sarah raised an eyebrow and folded her arms as she stared at him.

"Oh, whatever Sarah. That was twenty years ago."

"It's still weird."

"ANYWAY," he said, redirecting the conversation, "Melissa used to model for them in high school. Did some other stuff too, but that was her big thing. She was the reason I never missed Latin class."

"Were you even friends with her?"

"Hardly. I sometimes ended up being partnered with her for worksheets we had to do, though. She seemed pretty nice. I never really said that much. I was too busy making sure my erection wasn't showing."

"Some things never change," she said.

"What's that supposed to mean?" he asked.

"I mean like on Halloween when Carol came around with Marianne wearing that ridiculous French maid costume." Carol was a young, single mother living with her daughter Marianne two houses up in their townhouse community in Springfield. She'd explained her outfit by saying she was going to a party later, but Sarah hadn't bought it then or now.

"I don't know what you're talking about," he said. "That was nothing but a Kit Kat bar in my jacket pocket and some bad lighting."

"You weren't wearing a jacket."

"I wasn't?"

She shook her head slowly. "No, you weren't. And besides, she wasn't even wearing it right."

"Could have fooled me," he muttered.

She glanced at him and hopped off the couch, walking over to the hutch in the corner of the family room. Opening the bottom doors, she pulled out a light blue photo album and flipped through the photos. "Now this is how you wear a French maid costume," she said, closing the door with her foot and handing him the album as she sat on the arm of his chair. "Notice the feather duster matches the outfit."

He took it from her and coughed when he saw her picture. "When the hell was this taken?"

"It was junior year during my sorority Halloween party. I'm sure you've seen it before."

"Yeah, I think I'd remember that if I had. Can I keep this?" he asked as he pointed to the picture.

"You have the real thing, Jimmy," she said, taking the photo album back from him. He whimpered as she closed it. "How on earth did you ever get me to marry you?" she asked, shaking her head.

"I think I got you drunk on Southern Comfort and Mr. Pibb."

"No, that's just why I first went out with you," she said and smiled. "Why else would I have agreed to a date with someone sporting those ridiculous muttonchops?"

"Oh, that's right," he said, "but they were not muttonchops, they were sideburns, and they were hip."

"Of course they were. Now, are we done? I'd like to watch this interview."

"Yeah, sure, here you go," he said, handing her the remote and heading towards the stairs. "I gotta get ready for work anyway."

The house phone rang as Sarah settled into the couch. *Naturally*, she thought.

"Jim? Can you get that?" she asked.

The phone rang again as she waited for his acknowledgement. When none came, she dropped the remote and grabbed the phone from the counter. Charlotte's number appeared on the caller ID.

"Hey Char," she said. "You all set for—"

"Did you watch?" Charlotte asked. Charlotte Charles had been Sarah's best friend since college and even dated and eventually married one of Jim's close friends, Eric Dawkins.

"Not yet, I was just about to," she said. "But listen to this. Jim tells me this morning he went to high school with Beth's older sister."

"And he's never mentioned this before?"

"You know Jim. He couldn't even remember who Michele Groves was until I reminded him."

"I went through the same thing with Eric last night. We were—Sammy, put them down! Eric, would you get down here and get your son dressed, please?"

Sarah patted her neck and smirked as she listened to Charlotte's pleas for help. Sammy was Charlotte and Eric's eight-year-old son and had a horrible sweet tooth, even worse than Jim's.

"He's already driving me nuts," Charlotte said. "What time can you meet me over there?"

"Why don't I just get ready now and meet you there around 8:45. It's at Tyler Elementary, just off Shields Lane, right?"

"Exactly, just behind the high school. You can park—"

Sarah jerked her head away from the phone as a loud crashing sound came over the line.

"I'm sorry, Sarah, I gotta go. Sammy is running around knocking stuff everywhere. I'll see you soon, okay? Bye."

Charlotte hung up before Sarah could even say goodbye. When people wondered why she and Jim were thirty-five and still childless, she'd point to conversations like the one she just had. *Why would anyone want to deal with all that aggravation?* She shook her head and sighed as she downed the last few drops of her water bottle and placed it in the recycling bin before she went to turn off the TV. The image of Beth and Michele was still frozen on the set as she picked up the remote. Now free from Jim's vulgar distractions, she took in the picture and smiled. They were every bit as photogenic a pair as she'd remembered, and the story still touched her like few ever had.

"Oh, that's why," she whispered, turning it off and hurrying up the stairs.

2

"What the hell, Lisa? I can't get onto our system," Jim said as he banged the side of the terminal.

Lisa was the only one at the CRC regional dispatch office when Jim arrived shortly before 9 a.m. She could get away with her outfit on a Saturday morning, which consisted of a pink jogging suit and sneakers. Her strawberry blonde hair had been pulled back into a ponytail, and the glasses she had on were the same pair she complained two days earlier weren't strong enough.

"It'll be a minute. I just rebooted the machine before you came in," she said. She yawned and rested her head on the desk as she closed her bloodshot eyes.

"Jesus—were you up all night drinking or something?" he asked.

"Or something," she said. "I was helping with this all night dance-a-thon to raise money for children's cancer out in West Chester." She stretched and stifled another yawn. "You look surprised."

"Wow, no. I mean, that's great and all, just seems crazy to do that all night and then try and work this morning."

"I know. A bunch of us signed up awhile back right after the whole thing with Baby Michele. And we weren't the only ones who did that, apparently. They must have had ten thousand people show up—it was insane"

"And all these people showed because of that girl Michele?"

"It had to be. One woman got up and spoke about her four-year-old son who was in a wheelchair. She said when he saw the story about Michele on the news, he said to her, 'That's going to be me, Mommy. I'm going to be all better.' Of course the entire crowd is in tears at that point."

"Shut up—that didn't happen," he said. "You sure the kid's name wasn't Tiny Tim? Did he carve the roast beast too?"

"Wasn't that the Grinch?"

"I thought it was Tiny Tim."

Lisa waved him off. "Fine, mock all you want. But they're expecting to raise twenty-five million dollars by the time it's over tomorrow. That's four times as much as the previous high."

He shook his head as he logged into the terminal, which was now back online. "Man oh man. That kid's like a gold mine, and her mother isn't even cashing in on it. If it was me I'd slap that kid's face on every lunchbox and piece of crap knick-knack I could find."

"That's real nice. Ready to sell out the kid you don't even have yet," she said.

"What, if you're going to do interviews anyways, might as well get paid. You know they were on the *TODAY* show earlier?"

"I know, I was planning to watch when you left. Thanks again for rigging up my computer to stream video from that old DVR. Nobody else here could've gotten that to work."

"I'm amazing, aren't I?" he asked, blowing on his knuckles and polishing them against his chest. "I don't know how you're going to live without me."

"You're not really going to take that job in Texas, are you?" she asked as she walked over to the printer to collect his work orders. "There's no way Sarah's going to go for that."

"Sarah's not the boss of me," he said. "I can do whatever I want." Lisa tried but failed to stifle a laugh as she handed him the sheets from the printer. He asked, "And what are you sputtering at exactly?"

"Gee I wonder," she said. "So you've told Sarah you're taking the job then?"

"Well, I haven't said anything explicit yet," he said. "But that's the great thing about our marriage. I can just—" Lisa rolled her eyes as she picked up the phone on the counter and started dialing. "Who are you calling?" he asked.

"I'm calling Sarah to say goodbye since—"

Jim lunged forward and slammed his hand down on the receiver. "Are you crazy?" he asked. "Sarah would kill me."

"What's the matter? I thought you could do whatever you wanted."

"Oh you're a riot," he said. "Look, if I decide to take that job, I'll tell her in my own special way."

"Which is?"

"From the plane as I'm taking off."

"Exactly. Why don't you just forget about that stupid job and go full time here?" He'd seen the posting on the internal company website for full-time position at his dispatch office but hadn't bothered applying. While it meant a raise in pay and being eligible for company benefits, it also meant signing a minimum one-year contract, which the company had implemented to prevent new hires from getting thousands of dollars of training and then jumping to another company.

"I'm not sticking around here another year. And it's what, ten grand if I quit before my contract is up?"

"You're exaggerating," she said. "It's only 7500."

"Thanks, but no thanks," he said as he looked over the work orders. "I'll find something back in sales. Hey, this Paul Nelson guy in Villanova. Doesn't Derek play poker with a Paul Nelson?"

"Yeah, that's the same guy," she said as she went back to her seat.

"But it's a disconnect?"

She shrugged. "I guess he lost."

"Boy, guess so." He flipped to the next page and slammed his hand down on the counter as he read the address. "Why the hell am I getting sent all the way out to Exton?"

"Derek said you'd be thrilled with that," she said.

Exton was at least thirty-five minutes west of the office. "He realizes Exton's handled by another office, right?"

She nodded. "Derek told them you'd do it. You're supposed to do a signal leakage test for that place."

Conducting a signal test on people's cable connection was his least favorite part of the job. It was normally just an issue with something inside the house, but sometimes it meant there was cable theft involved. People generally weren't happy to see him around if they were stealing cable, and it was hard to do the test undetected with a marked van parked out front.

"No way, I'm not doing that," he said and put the pen down. "The last time I did that a guy came charging out of his house with a golf club and tried to take my head off."

"That's probably why Derek volunteered you."

He rubbed his face in frustration. "God I hate this fucking job."

"No you don't; you just hate Derek."

"I hate them both."

She shook her head and stretched. "No, you don't. I've seen you come in after your shift all happy you made some kid's day because they could watch *Elmo's World* on demand."

"You must be thinking of Francisco," he said as he came around the counter to her. "Just give me the form."

Lisa opened her desk drawer and handed him a blank site survey report form. "Call if you need anything," Lisa said. "Now get out of here before Derek shows up."

"Yeah, yeah," he said as he folded the papers and shoved them in his back pocket. "Make sure you give him a hug and tell him it's from me."

"Just get out and let me get some sleep."

He laughed and waved as he headed out.

* * *

It was 10:15 a.m. and the gym at Tyler Elementary swarmed with kids and their frazzled parents. The bake sale Sarah had volunteered for was only part of the school fair occurring that day to raise money for the PTO.

"How much for those?" the little girl asked.

"The cupcakes are seventy-five cents," Sarah said. The girl opened her hand and counted the change she had left.

"I only have fifty cents. Do you have anything I can get for that?"

"Are you sure you only have fifty cents?" Sarah asked, leaning over the table. The girl counted again as Sarah slipped her hand in her pocket. "Yeah, only fifty cents," the girl said.

"Well what about this here?" Sarah asked, and reached her hand behind the girl's ear to pull out another quarter.

The girl gasped and smiled as Sarah dropped it in her hand. "That was amazing! I didn't even know it was there." Sarah laughed and took the girl's money as she placed the cupcake on a napkin for her. The girl took it and skipped off towards the exit. Charlotte walked back from the area near the tumbling mats where Sammy stood in a long line.

"How's it going?" Charlotte asked.

"Fine. What's Sammy doing?" she asked, counting the remaining baked goods on the table and updating her self-made inventory sheet.

"He's getting his face painted like The Joker."

"The Joker? Isn't that going to take awhile?"

Charlotte nodded. "As long as it keeps him away from the food, he can stay in that line for as long as it'll take."

"What's with your 'The New Hollywood' t-shirt?" Charlotte asked.

Sarah straightened the bright pink shirt out and grinned. "It's this great women's group out in LA my cousin Angelia's in. She sent me the shirt and some other stuff as a birthday gift last month."

"Oh, I remember you telling me about her. How's her little boy doing?"

"He's good," she said. "Cute little guy, just started first grade this year."

"So . . .?" Charlotte nudged her.

"Here we go," Sarah said. "Why are you always so eager for me to have kids?"

"Because I think you'd be a great mom."

"You just want someone else to complain about their kids with you."

"Either way," Charlotte said as she shrugged. "But maybe then Jim would have less time to spend chatting with Carol and Marianne when they coming wandering by. What do you think he was really talking to her about?" Sarah had spotted Jim outside speaking to Carol earlier in the week when he thought she was in the shower. He'd told her about it only after she confronted him, and then struggled to explain what he was talking to Carol about.

"I don't know, but I don't like it," Sarah said as she adjusted the brownie arrangement.

"That woman is definitely trouble," Charlotte said. "I heard Eric describing her to one of his friends on the phone yesterday."

A woman and young boy wearing a tuxedo approached the table. The woman, a petite blonde in her late thirties, attractive and well-dressed, sipped from a diet soda can as they approached. The boy kept turning his head and looking at the entranceway to the gym.

"When's Dad getting here?" the boy asked.

"He'll be here soon, sweetheart. He's just busy at work," the woman said.

"Do you think he'll like the surprise?"

"I'm sure he'll love it, Christian. Now do you want anything from this table?"

"No, I want to wait until Dad gets here. Can I go do the ring toss?" The woman smiled and nodded as she took his hand. He looked back at the gymnasium door before they walked to the ring toss corner.

"What is with the kid in the tuxedo?" Sarah asked.

"That's Cal Nolan's kid Christian and his wife Bonnie. They come to all of these things."

"Ugh. You didn't tell me Cal Nolan might be here. I wouldn't have come," she said.

"I wouldn't worry about it too much. He never bothers showing up. That poor kid is wearing that dumb tuxedo for nothing."

"Aw, that's so sad. Why doesn't Cal come?"

"Probably knocking boots with a Knockout," Charlotte said, shaking her head as she watched Christian miss badly with his first ring.

"Really?" Sarah asked. "Do you think he's . . .?"

"No, I doubt it. I heard Bonnie only let him do the whole Nolan Knockout thing if he signed a post-nuptial agreement where if he commits adultery, he gets nothing in the divorce."

"Is that right? Hmm, my boss might enjoy hearing about that. He can't stand Cal either."

"I thought Cal was one of your firm's biggest clients?"

"He is, but I've never heard Mr. Donald say once nice thing about that guy," she said. Frank Donald, along with John Kim, founded the accounting firm Donald and Kim LLP almost forty years ago, and it was now one of the largest in the city. "It's been one complaint after another now that our firm is stuck gathering up records for that lawsuit against him. Thank god I'm not on that project."

Charlotte's phone rang, and she fumbled in her pants pocket to retrieve it.

"Is that Flock of Seagulls?" Sarah asked.

"Yeah, don't ask," she said. "You mind if I take this outside? Eric probably can't find the remote or something. Can you make sure Sammy doesn't wander off? "

"No problem, I'll keep an eye on him."

Charlotte ran out into the hallway as Sarah took a seat behind the table. People continued to wander by but weren't very interested in what items they had left. She pulled out her phone to calculate lower price points and potential profits based on each one.

"Hey, Hollywood. Where's the bathroom in this place?" a man's voice said. She recognized it from his commercials even before she looked up and swept her brown hair out of her face. Cal Nolan stood in front of the table, wearing a dark blue suit and a light blue tie. The Bluetooth headset in his ear flashed, and he gestured for her to hurry up with her answer.

"Excuse me?" she asked.

"Look, I'm in a hurry here, so can you point out where the bathrooms are or not?"

"They're over there," she said and pointed out their location. "And my name's not—"

"Thanks, Hollywood." He tapped his headset and took a cupcake from the tray before he headed off. "So, where was I?" he asked. "Right, advertising budget. So what do you think we—"

"Hey!" she yelled and scurried in front of him.

"Dammit, hold on." Cal tapped his headset and looked at her. "What do you want?"

"You took that cupcake without paying for it," she said, standing with her hands on her hips.

He dismissed her with a wave. "I'll pay for it later," he said and headed off again.

"No, you'll pay for it now," she said, sliding in front of him.

"Do you have any idea who you're talking to?"

"I don't care who you are. It's seventy-five cents for that cupcake."

He stroked his moustache and again tried to step around her. She folded her arms and blocked him once more. He tapped his headset to resume the call.

"Let me call you back," he said. He popped the earpiece out and typed something into his phone.

"What's your e-mail address, Hollywood?"

"Excuse me?"

"I'm sending you the money via Paypal, so I need an e-mail address or phone number."

"Is this a joke? This is a bake sale, we don't take Paypal."

"So you're refusing my payment for this cupcake?"

"Daddy!" Christian yelled, sprinting over to Cal. "Is that cupcake for me?"

"Well, look at you," Cal said, admiring his son's homage as he ran up. "It was, but I'm afraid this woman won't sell it to me."

"Why not?" Cal's wife asked as she walked up. She looked Sarah over and shook her head.

"You know how it is with some people, dear," Cal said. "They just can't get past the commercials."

"That's not what I—" Sarah said. Cal waved her off, handed the cupcake to Christian and walked back to the table. He then pulled out his money clip and peeled off a hundred dollar bill.

"I'm sorry you find me so offensive, miss," he said and set the money on the table. "But I'm sure you wouldn't want to hold that against a little boy now, would you? Keep the change." He came back and patted Christian on the head, giving him a big smile. "Bon-Bon, why don't you take Christian over to the dunk tank while I hit the head?"

"Yay," Christian cheered.

"That's fine, dear," Bonnie said. "We'll meet you over there. Let's go, Christian." She glared at Sarah as she took Christian's hand and marched off to the dunk tank.

"Bye, bye Hollywood," Cal said.

Sarah clenched her fists as Cal winked at her and headed to the bathroom.

"Did he just leave a hundred dollar bill?" Charlotte asked, hurrying back behind the table.

Sarah picked up the money and threw it in the cash box. "Yeah, but first he tried to steal a cupcake."

"He didn't!"

"Yes he did," she said. "I stopped him as he tried to walk off, and then he tried to pay for it via Paypal."

"Well, he gave us a hundred dollars. It all worked out in the end."

"For him it did. I'm still pissed."

"Calm down hon, there's not much left here for anyone to steal anyways. Look, why don't you go take a break? The fair is over in another hour and then maybe we can grab lunch or something. What time is Jim getting home?"

"I don't know, I was going to send him a text message," she said. "Let me go call him."

"Take your time. Sammy's still waiting in that line. I'll make sure Cal doesn't take another cookie."

"Cupcake!"

Charlotte laughed. "Okay, cupcake. Now go outside and try to relax."

Sarah took her phone to the parking lot where the fresh air and bright sunshine was a welcome change from the stuffy gymnasium.

"Hey babycakes. What's up?" Jim answered.

"Oh not much. Have I got a story for you, though."

"I hope it's not another story about how upsetting you found it that someone used Cocoa Krispies to make Rice Krispie squares," he begged.

"No, it's not that."

"Why did you go back?" he said. "The last time you helped Charlotte with this, you spent the whole week afterwards complaining about how much you hated it."

"The last bake sale was at her church. This one is at her kid's school."

"Church? What exactly does she consider church, Target?"

"You know she sometimes goes to—"

"Wal-mart? Best Buy? Costco?"

"Jim!"

"Right, sorry. Your spine-tingling story of the bake sale. Please proceed."

"Thank you," she said. "As I was saying, I'm here helping Charlotte and up walks Cal Nolan and—"

"Cal Nolan!" he said. "That's awesome! Did he have any of the Nolan Knockouts with him?"

"No, he didn't have any of the Nolan Knockouts with him. But guess what he—"

"Hey sweetie, hold on a sec." The line was quiet for a few seconds, although she thought she heard Jim turn the ignition off in his van.

"What are you doing?" she asked.

"I'm out in Exton doing a—hey, check it out! There's a Nolan Realty sign in the front window."

"Of course there is," she said. "Look, I'm going to go. I'm pretty sick of Cal Nolan and Nolan Realty."

"But I thought you wanted to tell me something."

"Forget it. You want me to bring home something for lunch?"

"Maybe. Depends where you're going."

"I'm guessing we'll go to Popper's Deli."

"Sweet. Yeah, that'd be great. Can you pick me up a Nolan Special Hoagie and some chips?"

"Are you trying to piss me off?" she asked. "Cause if you are—"

"I'm serious," he said. "They added it to the menu like two weeks ago. They donate ten percent of the purchase price to local soup kitchens to help knockout hunger. It's really good."

"I don't believe this," she said. "I've done charity work for years to help feed the homeless and—" She stopped herself and realized what she was about to say. No matter how much she loathed Cal Nolan, she wasn't going to make someone go hungry because of it. "Alright, one Nolan Special Hoagie," she said. "In fact I'll get one too. What's on it exactly?"

"Um, chicken breast, turkey breast—"

"I get the idea. I'll see you when you get home."

"Sounds like a plan. Love you."

"Love you too. Bye."

She hung up the phone and laughed. *Unbelievable*, she thought. There was a group of smokers now congregated by the door she'd gone out, so she headed around the side to re-enter through the main entrance. A black BMW was parked in the handicapped spot closest to the door.

KNOK-OUT, the plate read.

Ugh, she thought and stomped back inside.

3

As Jim hung-up with Sarah, he got out of his van and stood in front of the unimpressive house at 714 Timothy Court, which was hidden from the cul-de-sac because of a long driveway that sloped down into a wooded valley. Traffic from the nearby turnpike created a kind of soothing white noise in the background while he looked the place over. It was an older, two-story building with a red exterior, black shutters, and white door. There was some furniture inside, but it didn't appear to be fully furnished. A staircase led up the side of a detached garage to an apparent in-law suite.

He walked over to peer in the garage. Seeing no cars were inside, he relaxed a bit. The CRC cable junction box was attached to the main house against the wall opposite the garage. The contract every CRC customer signed when they received new service prohibited tampering with the box and allowed company employees to check it at any time with or without warning.

The cause of the signal leakage was obvious. The box door had been jimmied open, and the cable line coming from the road was split using a component from Radio Shack. One line now fed into the house while the other had been run up into the in-law suite above the garage.

"Hey Lisa, you there?" Jim asked, flipping open his phone and activating the walkie-talkie function.

No response.

"Lisa?"

"Hey Jim, I'm here," she said. "Sorry, Derek is fighting with the snack machine guy. What's up?"

"I'm at this stupid house in Exton. This Doug Flynn guy just ran a line over to the in-law suite above his garage. It's not a big deal. The wiring looks fine, but the splitter isn't ours, and he opened the box up. Can you ask Derek want he wants me to do?"

"Is the guy there?"

"No. In fact, there's a Nolan Realty sign in the window and no cars in the garage, so I don't even know if the guy is still living here," he said.

"Knox!" Derek said, apparently having heard their conversation and grabbed Lisa's walkie. "You just say there's a Nolan Realty sign in the window?"

"Yeah, so what?"

The line was silent. He looked at the time on his phone, which said 11:00 a.m. *Maybe I can get home early*, he thought. "Derek? Lisa? Hello?"

"Pull the line from the garage and cap the line into the main house," Derek said. "Then file a theft report with the CRC main office."

"What? Are you crazy?"

"The in-law suite is a separate residence, and therefore it's cable theft."

Jim ran his fingers through his hair and shook his head. "Dude, I'm just calling it an in-law suite. There's nothing to suggest that it's actually being used as a separate residence. It's not like there's a sign on the wall that says 'The Fonz' with an arrow pointing upstairs."

"You keep crackin' wise with me Knox, and I'll bounce your ass. Just do it and shut the hell up for once."

"Don't you think you're overreacting to all this?"

"Knox, pull the fucking line, or I'll pull your fucking job. Any other questions?"

The phone beeped off, and Jim threw up his hands. He puffed his cheeks and looked at the connection.

"Fine, whatever," he muttered. He needed his ladder to cut both ends of the connection running into the garage suite, so he trudged to his van and set about unhooking the ladder from it.

A blue Porsche zoomed down the driveway with a Nolan Realty plate on the front of the car. He forgot all about the ladder as the car pulled into the turnaround space and out of the Porsche stepped a jaw-dropping woman. She was in her mid-twenties with sandy blonde hair and brown eyes. Her outfit, a blue jacket over a black mini-dress that showed off her long legs, was completed with shiny, black leather sling-back pumps that looked expensive.

"That's right, Jane Scanlon. Scan-lon," she said into the phone as she walked up to him. "Yes, I'll hold." She pulled up her sunglasses and looked him over as she covered the phone with her left hand, which had an inch long scar on the back. "What's the cable company doing out here?"

"Yeah, uh, you see, there was this leak, with the signal, and I had to come check it out. Is Mr. Flynn going to be home later today, or does he still live here? Because I have to cap—"

"Yes, I'm still here," she said into the phone. "Fine, then transfer me. Thank you."

She sighed before she spoke to Jim. "Look, I'm kind of in the middle of something here. Can whatever you need to do wait until tomorrow? I'm sure it can be straightened out then."

"Well, I have pretty strict instructions—"

"Please?" She flipped her hair to the side and tilted her head. "It would mean so much to me."

He swallowed hard as he looked at her pouty full lips. "Yep, tomorrow's no problem. Someone will be here around noon?"

She nodded and smiled. "That'll work." She walked over and unlocked the front door with a key from her pocket, disappearing inside as she waved.

God bless Cal Nolan, he thought. After making sure the ladder was re-secured, he pulled up the driveway and punched an address into the GPS. He called Lisa back on the regular office line as he drove off.

"CRC Dispatch, this is Lisa," she answered.

"Hey, it's Jim."

"What are you doing calling this number?"

"I don't want Derek to know you're talking to me. Is he around?"

"He's back in his office. Why, what are you up to?"

"The realtor showed up and asked me to come back tomorrow. I guess the owner will be back then."

"So you didn't finish?" she asked. "Are you crazy? Derek's going to kill you when he finds out."

"Look, the report doesn't need to be filed until Monday, so if I talk to the owner tomorrow, I can straighten this out and save this guy from being raked over the coals by Derek for something stupid."

"Listen to you. This morning you're all . . . wait a minute, there was a Nolan Realty sign in the window and the realtor shows up? Well, I guess we know where you suddenly found your can of spinach."

"I'm just a nice guy," he protested.

"Yeah, a nice, unemployed guy if he's not careful. Fine, you do what you want. But you're playing with fire."

"Don't worry about me," he said. "Just tell Derek I'm faxing over the report to the main office when I get home. Besides, I've always got Texas to fall back on."

"I'll tell him," Lisa said. "Anything else, Tex?"

"Nope, I gotta run. I guess I'll talk to you tomorrow?"

"Actually, I'm—"

The call dropped as Jim turned onto the main highway, heading towards a large outdoor shopping center. After a ten minute drive, he pulled into the lot of Goodman's Shoe Warehouse and parked the van. He'd only ever been to the large store once before and didn't remember it being so busy. The number of choices was overwhelming.

"Hi, welcome to Goodman's Shoe Warehouse," the greeter said as he entered. "Can I help you find something today?"

"Yes," he said. "Yes, you can."

*　*　*

It was just after 1:30 p.m. when she got home from lunch with Charlotte. She found Jim sprawled out on the couch watching football and flipping through a *Fitness Magazine*.

"Alright, sandwich time!" he said, tossing the magazine aside and hurrying over to her.

"Nice to see you too," she said and handed him the bag.

"Oh right, hi babe," he said and kissed her on the cheek. "Hey, how come you're not wearing the shirt I left out for you?"

"Are you kidding? Did you really think I'd wear a Texas Longhorns shirt?" She took off her shoes and fell into the couch.

"Well, it's nicer than that kooky shirt you're wearing," he said as he unwrapped his sandwich. "What's so great about 'The New Hollywood' anyway? Just because it's new doesn't mean it's better. I mean, look at New Coke."

"You loved New Coke! You cried when the Acme finally stopped selling it."

"Hmm, good point. Speaking of New Coke, you want something to drink? I picked up some Yoo-Hoo on the way home," he said and headed into the kitchen.

"Well, thank you for finally taking care of that list," she said. "Did they have the type of ginger ale I like?"

He stopped at the fridge and smacked his forehead as he looked at the list of items she wanted him to pick up, still pinned to the black freezer door with a "Don't Forget" magnet shaped like an apple. "Oh right, the list," he said. "I probably should have brought this with me."

"Are you telling me you went the grocery store and only bought a six pack of Yoo-Hoo?"

"No, I bought two six packs," he said. "It was buy one, get one free. Oh, and I got a bottle of mustard."

"Well naturally," she said. "Because nothing goes with Yoo-Hoo quite like some delicious mustard. Do you realize how many jars of mustard we have in the cabinet already?"

"Eight, but we didn't have the jalapeño kind."

She looked at the time and stood up. "Just give me the list and I'll go myself. There's some stuff I—"

"No, don't you dare," he said. "That'd mean I was back on vacuum patrol, and I'm never going through that hell again."

"Vacuum patrol was not that bad an assignment. It should have taken you twenty minutes."

"Not with you following me around and telling me to use eighteen different attachments to do one room. Forget it, I did my time in the hole, and now I'm out. I earned store duty through my blood and my sweat and my blood and—"

"Knock it off. You better do it soon then, or you'll think vacuum patrol was a cakewalk compared to laundry brigade."

"Lost some good men on the laundry brigade. God rest their souls."

He crossed himself as she giggled. "Okay, I won't take your beloved store duty from you. But I would take a Diet Coke from you if we have one," she said and sat back in her seat.

"Yep, got one more." He returned with a can of Diet Coke and handed her the soda as he sat next to her and tore into his sandwich. The sandwich oil dripped out of the bottom of the hoagie roll and splashed onto the black leather of the sofa.

"Do you see the mess you're making?" she asked. He looked down and saw the oil spill, which he proceeded to wipe with his shirt sleeve. She walked to the kitchen sink and got some paper towels and cleaning supplies.

"Go eat that at the table. My god, you're worse than Sammy."

He gathered his assorted items without objection and hurried to the table to continue his feeding frenzy. The sandwich was gone in three more of his monstrous bites while she cleaned up the oil stain he'd left behind. She set the paper towel roll in front of him and shook her head in amazement.

"What the hell got into you? You wolfed down that sandwich like you were Shaggy or something."

"Shaggy?"

"Sorry," she said, "Guess I have *Scooby-Doo* on the brain. Must have seen a half-dozen kids wearing *Scooby-Doo* t-shirts today."

"No, it's fine, I love Shaggy," he said. "I just get sick of dealing with Derek's bullshit sometimes, that's all."

"He's just trying to get your goat," she said, pulling a chair up to the table.

"Well, he's got it," he said. "Besides, I'm tired of this job anyway. I never thought I'd even be at CRC this long. I should've never gone to that stupid start-up." Before beginning work with CRC sixteen months ago, he'd been let go from a folding start-up company where he sold business software packages. One of the companies he pitched the system to was CRC, and while they didn't buy it, the people he met liked him and said if he was ever looking for a job to give them a call. When he finally did call, a service technician position was the only job open. He'd had some experience in the field from work he did in college installing satellite dishes, so he jumped on what he'd hoped was temporary work before getting back into sales.

She pulled her chair closer to him. "You were miserable at that job. And at every job before that. You're great at this and most days you seem to like it."

"Are you implying I wasn't great at my other jobs?" he asked as he leaned back in his chair.

"It's not that you weren't good at them," she said. "They just weren't you. This job seems to make you happy. You get to help people, you love driving that silly van around, and you're home most nights, which never happened when you were traveling all the time."

"What is with everyone today, trying to tell me how happy I am at this stupid job?" he asked. "I didn't go to college to spend my life working as a cable installer. I need to get back into sales and that job in Texas—"

"You're not taking that job in Texas, period," she said and moved her chair back a bit. "So quit bringing it up. I'm sure you can find something around here if you really want to leave CRC."

"Like what? I've been looking for over a year now and nothing's come along."

"I don't know, maybe I could check with Mr. Donald if there's anything—"

"No way," he said. He crumpled up his trash and threw it over his shoulder into the trash can. "Like it isn't bad enough you're already making more money than me, now I need you to get a job for me too?"

"Is that what this is really all about?" she asked. "The fact I have a higher salary than you?"

"I don't know, maybe," he said. He chugged the last bit of Yoo-Hoo and tossed the bottle in the recycling bin. "I guess Cal Nolan didn't mention if he was looking for male Knockouts, did he?"

She crushed her empty soda can in her hands. "No, we didn't really do the small talk thing when he stopped by."

"Yeah, so tell me what happened with him exactly?"

She retold the events of the bake sale while Jim looked around the room and sighed. Sarah included a detailed description of the gym's layout and approximate number of attendees. Jim went into a mock snoring routine when she described the type of sprinkles on the cupcake Cal had stolen.

"C'mon, Jim," she said.

"Look Hollywood, just get to—"

"Don't even start with that."

"I get it, you think Cal Nolan's a jerk, and you have ever since he fired all of those realtors and only hired hot women," he said. "But the Temple game is on at two o'clock, and I don't want to miss the start of it."

"So you don't think what he did was wrong?"

"It was just a cupcake."

"I meant about firing the realtors."

He shrugged. "Not really, I mean, it's his business, so as long as everything he did was legal, then who cares? Would you want anyone telling you how to run your business?"

"No," she said. "But I also wouldn't fire everyone who worked for me just so I could go from being rich to super-rich. Those poor people deserved better than that. A lot of them are still looking for work."

"Then get your own real estate company up and running and you can hire all of them," he said as he walked over to pick up the remote from the coffee table. "Or maybe they'd be interested in the opportunities that are currently available at a certain sporting goods distributor in Texas. I know I certainly am."

"You know what wise guy? Just for that, you've volunteered for leaf duty with your wife this afternoon." She snatched the remote from his hand and settled into the couch.

"Oh, c'mon. I hate leaf duty."

"How do you know?" she asked. "You've never volunteered before."

"I read the brochures the recruiter left, and it wasn't for me. At least let me watch the first half before I report for duty."

"Here, I'll make a deal with you. Watch this interview with me, and you can watch the whole Temple game before you have to come outside," she said. She pulled up the list of recorded programs, which was almost exclusively filled with Jim's favorite shows. There were four episodes of *Psych*, eight episodes of *Jeopardy*, and five episodes of *The Simpsons*. She found the *TODAY* show in the list that contained the interview with Beth Groves and queued it up.

"Well, who's doing the interview—Lester Holt or Amy Robach? I'm only watching if it's Amy."

"Sit. Down," she ordered. "Or would you rather grab a rake right now?"

"Lester's not so bad," he said and sat down next to her. She hit play and set the remote out of Jim's reach. He pumped his fist when he saw Amy was on the screen.

"Beth, thank you so much for speaking with us today."

"Thank you, Amy. We're happy to be back."

"So, the obvious question. How is Michele doing?"

"Michele's doing wonderfully," Beth said, looking a little nervous as she rubbed her daughter's back. "She's a special little girl."

"And there's no sign of the disease, of the Spinal Muscular Atrophy she'd been diagnosed with?"

"None. The doctors have told me they expect she'll grow up to be a perfectly healthy and happy little girl."

"Can you explain what it felt like when they told you that?"

"It's, it's really indescribable to have the same people who just a few days earlier said there was no hope, to then say everything will be okay. I mean, it was just so incredibly amazing."

"Now some in the medical community say that they feel her diagnosis must have been wrong. That since there's no known cure for SMA that it was something else that was missed along the way. Do you think that's a possibility?"

"Not at all, Amy. You know, I think people sometimes are just looking to, uh, to assign blame no matter what happens if they can't explain something. Michele's doctors did everything in their power, and they were all so incredibly helpful, and sometimes you have something like this that no one can explain and people think, oh the doctors did something wrong. I'd rather focus on the positive than try and find a negative."

"You've obviously heard Michele's recovery called a miracle. We called it that in our tease for this segment before the break. Do you personally think it was a miracle, Beth?"

"You can, people can call it what they'd like. I have my little girl, and I'm not worried about what to call it."

"Are you happy Michele's story has contributed to a large rise in charitable donations and people volunteering to help other children in need?"

"I think that's one of the best things to come out of this entire saga with Michele. The fact that she's inspired so many people to give some of their time and hard-earned money when we're all facing these tough economic times is truly heartwarming, and we're very touched."

"Is that why you've made the decision not to try and profit off of her story?"

"My daughter has been through so much already, I just, as a mother, didn't feel comfortable putting her out there like some sort of a uh, prop in an ad or a movie or something like that. I'm just glad she's alive and has inspired so many already and that's the important thing."

"We all know your husband Steve died fighting in Afghanistan just a month before Michele was born," Amy said. "Has this experience with Michele made his passing any easier to deal with?"

"In some ways it's made things easier because I see things I loved about Steve in Michele. But I still struggle with his death and how much I wish I could have him on this journey with me."

"Do you have any advice for people going through a similar situation with their child? What would you say to them?"

Beth rubbed her left earring and shook her head. "I wouldn't want any other mother to have to go through that pain. It's so—" Beth looked at her little girl and started to tear up. "I'm sorry, just being here with her I can't believe I almost—" She collected herself and took a deep breath. "There's a reason I turn down these types of things."

"It's alright if you—"

"No, I'm fine, it's just," she said, glancing at Michele. "It's just I would try to stay positive and keep um, keep on working with the doctors, and just be there for your son or daughter as best you can and keep fighting the good fight."

"Okay, Beth Groves, thanks so much for taking the time and helping to give hope to so many around the country and the world. We really do appreciate it."

"Thank you, Amy," Beth said.

"And we're looking forward to seeing you on your first birthday there, cutie pie," Amy said as she shook the little girl's hand. Michele giggled as they shook.

"She's just adorable," Amy said. "Well, coming up next on *TODAY*, you love your cat, but does your cat really love you? We'll speak with a man who says—"

Sarah clicked off the interview and switched to the beginning of the football game for Jim. She sighed and got up to head upstairs. "Wasn't that sweet? I just can't imagine—"

He was rubbing his eyes, and he turned away when she looked at him.

"Oh my god, you're crying aren't you?" she asked.

"No I'm not."

"Then why won't you look at me?"

"I'm just tired of looking at your shirt, that's all."

"You're not fooling me. You've always been a big softie at heart. Just like when you helped that little girl on Route 30 a few years ago." Sarah had never forgotten a trip to the Jersey Shore they'd made four years ago where Jim saw a nine-year-old girl from their neighborhood standing unsteadily on bright white roller skates in the turning lane. Her older sister was jumping up and down in the 7-Eleven parking lot across the street, waving at her petrified sibling to come over. No one else stopped to help, so Jim pulled into the turning lane and shielded the girl from oncoming traffic. They picked up both her and her sister, bought them both Slurpees, and drove them back home to their mother.

"I can't help it," he said. "Something about a seeing a little girl crying, it gets me every time."

"Michele wasn't crying."

"Well, she was about to!"

"You are too much," she said, "Are you going to keep it together when you see the flower girls at Mark's wedding tomorrow?"

Mark and Jim had once been college roommates, and while Mark had attended their wedding ten years ago, the guys had drifted apart. Jim had been pretty surprised when he got the invitation. He was going to decline until Sarah found it in the trash can.

"I'm more worried about missing the Eagles game tomorrow. Who the hell schedules their wedding on a Sunday?"

"It's the anniversary of the day they met," she said.

"Lame," he mumbled.

"Lame or not, I still have to figure out what I'm wearing. It's supposed to be cooler out."

"Oh, that reminds me!" he said and jumped off the couch. "Sit back down for a second. I'll be right back."

He grabbed her shoulders and set her back on the couch before he ran upstairs. She cringed when she heard a loud thump from their bedroom.

"What was that?" she yelled.

"Um, nothing," he said, hustling down the stairs and coming back in the room to stand behind the couch. "Now close your eyes."

"It's too late for that. I already saw the shoebox."

"Oh, well, here you go then."

She took the gift from him as he leaned over the back of the couch. She gasped and pulled out a pair of brand new black leather sling-back pumps and put them on. They were a perfect fit.

"Do you like them? I thought you could wear them to the wedding tomorrow."

"Do I like them? Jimmy, I love them! " she said as she walked around on the hardwood floor and modeled them for him. She loved how they made her legs look.

"Good, I'm glad. I wanted to get something special for you."

The heels clicked as she came over to his spot behind the couch and kissed him on the lips. "It was very sweet, thank you. But what brought all this on?"

"Nothing. I just wanted to do something special for my wife, that's all."

Her eyes narrowed when she heard this. "You did, huh?" she asked. "Did you see Carol wearing these or something?"

"No, of course not," he said. "Stop being so suspicious all the time."

"The last expensive gift you bought me out of the blue was my engagement ring."

"That's ridiculous," he said. "And it's just a gift. Quit trying to ruin it."

"Mmmhmm," she said. "I swear, if I start asking around and find out you saw Carol wearing these . . ."

"I didn't see them on Carol, sheesh. Why do you always try and make everything a big mystery? It's like being married to Daphne."

"Daphne?"

"The hot chick from *Scooby-Doo*?"

"I know who Daphne is, and she never solved anything on that show. I always thought of myself more as a Velma."

"Velma couldn't pull off those heels," he said. "Now can I watch my football game, please?"

"By all means." She gestured for him to sit down on the couch, which prompted him to instead take a spot on the recliner.

"But if you're lying," she warned. "I'm going break off a piece of that Kit Kat bar." Jim swallowed hard as she turned and headed up the stairs.

4

"Where the hell is this place?" she asked, resting her head on her hand and leaning on the door. "You programmed the address into the GPS and then didn't even follow the route it told you."

"That way was dumb," he said. "This way is much faster." He'd thought the wedding didn't start until three when he agreed to return to the Exton house on Sunday, but that was the time of the reception, not the ceremony. Since the ceremony started at 1:30 and was much closer to Exton than from their home in Springfield, they were forced to stop on the way there. As he raced along the winding back roads, the potholes grew larger and became more frequent, and with each bump in the road, Sarah's sighs grew louder and louder.

"Why do you even bother using the GPS if you're never going to actually follow it?"

"Oh you're exaggerating. I followed it here yesterday for work. And I know I've followed it with you in the car before."

"Name one time."

"Well, what about that time we were meeting your entire family at your uncle's place in the Poconos?"

She shot him a look. "Gee, I forgot about the time you used it to find the longest route possible, so you'd barely have to spend any time actually talking to them. We missed most of dinner because you wouldn't use a toll road."

"But you were in the car, and I did follow it."

"I swear to god, Jim, I'm not in the mood right now."

"Look, it's not my fault we had to stop at the store because you ripped your pantyhose getting in the car."

"What do you mean, it isn't your fault?"

"How is that possibly my fault? They're your pantyhose," he said. "Maybe if you took less than two hours to do your hair for this stupid wedding you would have had all the time you needed to rip them and get a new pair."

"I wouldn't have been rushing around for any of it if we didn't have to stop at this god-forsaken house!"

"You know, this wouldn't be an issue if I had that job in—"

"Don't you dare say the word Texas!"

He said nothing for a minute before he started whistling the tune of "Deep in the Heart of Texas." She smacked him on the arm.

"What, I didn't say that word, did I?" he asked. She rolled her eyes as he turned onto the street towards the house. He pulled down the driveway and parked in front of the garage. There were no other cars in the driveway, but several lights were on inside the house.

"Look, you're the one who wants me to keep this job," he said as he exited the car. "So just wait here and let me help this guy out. It isn't going to take more than a couple minutes."

"Oh, spare me the good Samaritan routine. You're only back here because the realtor made goo-goo eyes at you. Did you bring a Kit Kat bar for her too?"

"Jane did not make 'goo-goo eyes' at me. She just asked—"

"Jane?" she asked. "So you're on a first name basis with a No-lan Knockout now, are you?"

"Would you knock it off, Sarah? Sheesh," he said. "First Carol and now this. Why are you so jealous?"

"I'm not jealous," she protested, folding her arms.

"Look at you, you are jealous! Ha, ha, you love your husband, you love your husband," he chanted like a child while dancing around in a circle. Before she could respond, he caught his shoe on the edging of the driveway, and he turned his ankle, which caused him to fall down. He lay there momentarily, humiliated but uninjured.

"Little help?" he asked feebly, reaching an arm towards the car.

Sarah got out and walked over to him lying in a pathetic heap. She stifled a laugh and extended her hand to help him up. "Are you okay?" she asked.

He rose to his feet and brushed off his pants, wishing his ego could be as easily repaired. "Yeah, I'm fine. I guess I deserved that."

"You think?"

"Fine, I definitely deserved that," he said. "That doesn't mean it's not silly for you to get jealous."

"Oh, I shouldn't? Between Carol and this woman batting her eyelids to get you to come back, it's just—"

"I'm the first to admit I'm a sucker for a pretty girl," he said. "But for whatever reason, every one of them seems to have this major flaw I can't get past."

"And what's that, their boobs are too big?"

"No," he said as he pulled her close, "It's just none of them are you." He kissed her on the forehead. "Now wait here, I'll be right back."

He bounded up to the door and rang the doorbell. After a few moments, he pushed it again, and there was still no response.

"There's no one home, is there?" she asked. He looked at her and smiled as he tried knocking this time. "CA-BLE GUYYYYY!" he said, doing his terrible Jim Carrey impression.

"Yeah great, Jim. Never gets old. Would you come on?" she said.

"Stupid, sexy Jane," he muttered, giving up and heading to the side of the house to disconnect the cable. "Hey, can you grab that bag in the trunk and bring it over to me please?" he asked.

"What for?" she asked, opening the door to pop the trunk.

"I just have to do something to this box real quick and then we can go. Not sitting around here waiting for Doug Flynn."

She retrieved his bag and walked it over to him. A black BMW zipped down the driveway and pulled in beside them. Jim heard Sarah's groan as they saw who was driving through the tinted windshield.

"Are you kidding me?" she asked.

"Holy shit, is that Cal Nolan? Man, this Flynn guy must be pretty important for Cal to come out personally."

Cal stepped out of the car and closed the door. He was impeccably dressed and checked his hair in the driver's side window before he strode over to them, grinning. Jim thrust his hand out to greet him.

"Jim Knox, CRC cable. I have to say, Mr. Nolan, it truly is a pleasure to meet you," he said.

"Please, Jim, call me Cal," Cal said as they shook. He started to shake Sarah's hand when he stopped and squinted as he looked her over. "Do I know you?" Cal asked.

Sarah rolled her eyes. "We just met yesterday. I'm—"

Cal snapped his fingers and pointed at her. "Hollywood! Of course. Didn't expect to see you again."

"Ha! Hollywood, that's great," Jim said, while she stared daggers at both of them. "Yeah, this is my wife, Sarah. I, uh, heard you two had a bit of a misunderstanding at a bake sale yesterday?"

"It's already forgotten," Cal said, tugging at his shirt sleeves.

"Oh it is, is it?" she asked.

"Absolutely. There's no need for you to apologize. Everyone makes mistakes."

"I made the mistake? You know what? You are—"

"Excuse us for a moment," Jim said, taking her arm and walking back towards the car. "What the hell are you doing?" he asked.

"What am I doing? I'm about to tell that cupcake-stealing asshole exactly what I think of him and his stupid Knockouts."

"You know how much money he spends on advertising with CRC? If you piss him off, I'll be fired and on the 9 a.m. flight to Austin tomorrow because of some bake sale. So I suggest you keep quiet."

Sarah kept looking over at Cal while Jim spoke. Jim turned and watched Cal pacing back and forth, checking his Blackberry. Every so often he'd grin and type something before sliding the unit back into his pocket.

"Who do you think he's texting?" she asked.

"Are you serious? Look, just go wait in the car, and I'll be done in a couple minutes."

"No way," she said, grabbing his hand as he tried to walk away. "I want to hear exactly what your buddy Cal is saying. I'm not going anywhere."

"You don't think he'll find it odd you're crushing my hand and won't leave my side?" he said, grimacing.

"I don't care what he finds odd, just tell him we're in love or something."

"I'm leaning towards 'or something' since my hand is turning blue. C'mon, let go, would ya? I don't care if you want to eavesdrop but try not to say anything."

"Fine," she said and released her grip. "But if he calls me Hollywood one more time . . ."

He shook his hand out a few times as they headed back. "I'm sorry about all that," Jim said. "I guess you can tell we're on our way to something else, and it's been a stressful morning. Anyway, I'm not sure what Jane told you about all this, but—"

"Jane?" Cal asked.

"Yeah, Jane Scanlon, the realtor that was here yesterday?"

Cal coughed and shook his head. "Oh, of course, Ms. Scanlon. No, uh, Jane didn't elaborate on why you were here yesterday. She just said there was some sort of problem, so I wanted to take care of this personally to make sure there were no issues selling the home."

"Wow, okay, that's really nice of you to help Mr. Flynn out like that," Jim said.

"There's a reason Nolan Realty is number one in customer satisfaction. We like to take a hands-on approach with all our customers."

Sarah cleared her throat as Jim led the way to the cable box at the base of the house.

"Well, let me show what this guy did then," Jim said and proceeded to explain the company regulations that'd been broken and Derek's threats to file the report for suspected cable theft. He told Cal how unreasonable Derek was being, and that the only thing standing between Mr. Flynn and federal prison was Jim.

"Jim, I can't tell you how much I appreciate you coming back here today. I think we can clear up this whole mess right here and now. Can you hold on a sec?" Cal pulled out his Bluetooth headset and popped it in his ear before he dialed. "John Matthews, please. Tell him Cal's calling."

"Who's John Matthews?" Sarah whispered.

"Um, if it's who I think it is, he's the chairman of CRC."

"John? Cal Nolan here. The fish biting up there?" Cal laughed at whatever was said. "Well John, I wanted to let you know about a situation that's come up with one of my client's homes here in

Exton. Apparently he broke a couple minor CRC policies, and some gung-ho manager wants to make a federal case out of the whole thing. I have a technician named Jim Knox here who's trying to clear things up, but he can't because of—Sure, I'll put him on." He tapped a button on the handset and handed the phone to Jim. "John Matthews for you."

Be cool, Jim thought as he took the phone from Cal.

"Yeah, hi, this is Jim Knox," he said.

"You know who this is, Mr. Knox?" John asked.

"Yes sir, I do."

"Then listen to me very carefully. You do whatever you need to do to make Mr. Nolan happy. Is that clear?"

"Absolutely, but my manager—"

"Doesn't spend millions with us every year. Who's your manager anyway?"

"Derek Sands."

"I'll have my assistant deal with Mr. Sands regarding this matter. You just take care of Mr. Nolan. Understood?"

"You can count on me, sir."

"Good. Unless you have anything further . . ."

"Nope, here you go." Jim handed the phone back to Cal. The conversation was over even before the handset was back in his pocket.

"How long will it take you to fix this?" Cal asked.

"Depends on what you want me to do. I can replace the splitter in about five minutes, but to re-string—"

"Five minutes is good. I have to make another call, so I'm going to step inside for a few minutes. Just knock if Hollywood there needs to fix her face." He unlocked the door to the house and stepped inside.

"What is that supposed—"

"She'll be fine," Jim said, leading her away from the door to retrieve his bag.

Sarah pretended to strangle Cal as she watched the door close. "Oh, I'm gonna kill that guy."

"Relax, it's over. Man, I thought I was going to piss my pants when he put Matthews on the phone," he said. He took a splitter from his bag and got to work.

"I don't get it," she said, still glaring at where Cal had gone inside. "Why's he so eager to help this guy Flynn out?"

"Well, he said he takes a hands-on approach."

"Calling the CEO of the cable company during his fishing trip to clean this up for a client? Don't you think that's a bit much?"

"Hey, if you have the power to pull strings, what's the point if you never pull them? Plus he got Derek in trouble. So Jimmy Crack Corn and I don't care." He finished installing the new splitter after three or four minutes passed and clapped his hands together like a blackjack dealer when he finished.

"What the hell was that?" she asked.

"Something I do after every job I finish. It's fun."

"So you do enjoy this job?"

"No, I just—"

Cal was grinning as he slammed the door and walked outside. He straightened his tie and smoothed his hair as he came over to them.

"We good?" Cal asked.

"Yep, good to go," Jim said.

"Walk with me for a moment before you go, Jim," he said, putting his hand around Jim's shoulder. "I'm sure your wife doesn't mind if we talk privately." He didn't wait for a response as he pulled Jim away from Sarah and headed off. They looked back at her as they talked quietly, although Jim was more nervous that she hadn't objected than if she'd done so.

"Is Hollywood back there always so smothering?" Cal asked. "That would drive me nuts. I don't know how you put up with her."

"Nice gams," Jim said.

Cal chuckled and nodded in agreement as he looked her over while she typed into her phone. "I gotta say, now that I've had a chance to really size her up, I'm pretty fucking impressed with the whole package. Was she always hot, or did you find her in the fatty discount bin and luck out after putting in your time during the chubby years?"

"She's uh, she's always been hot," he said, tugging at his collar. "In fact, when we met she was training to be in a fitness contest where you parade around in a sparkly bikini."

"Now see, most guys wouldn't have the balls to ask a chick like that out. But you saw her and said to yourself, I want to be the guy smearing the oil on that tight little body."

"Um, I think I was actually saying 'Don't throw up on her when you say hello.'"

Cal laughed and slapped him on the back, "I hear you, I hear you. I have to say, you aren't like the typical half-wit CRC sends to my house. Why is a guy like you wasting his time in such a shitty job?"

"It's really just a temporary thing. I'm actually in software sales, but my last company folded, and I'm uh, still waiting for the right opportunity to come along? Guess that's the best way to put it."

"Well why didn't you say so? I'm on the board of directors at TBQ Software. In fact, I've got a meeting over there on Tuesday."

TBQ was one of the largest business software companies in the world, and their headquarters was located fifteen minutes from Jim's house. He'd been trying for months to get an interview only to be stonewalled each time. Their base salary for the sales force was twice what he made at his last job, and the average commissions someone pulled in could push his total compensation close to 250,000 dollars.

"Tell you what," Cal said, "You did right by me for helping me avoid a headache with CRC, so why don't I get you setup with an interview over there. I'm sure there's a spot for you in the TBQ family."

"Wow, I don't know what to say."

"Don't say anything, it's the least I can do. Here, write your number on this," Cal said, handing him a business card with his information on one side and a family portrait on the other.

"This is quite a card," Jim said, jotting his number down and handing it back.

"I printed these up for my biggest clients. The number on it is one of those Google Voice numbers, and it rings every phone I have."

"Oh no way, you got one of those?" Jim asked.

"My wife saw a whole segment on the *TODAY* show about it awhile back and asked me to get it. She got tired of dialing multiple numbers when she'd try to reach me. I don't give it out to the hoi polloi." He looked back at Sarah, who was still working on her phone. He gave Jim another card from the stack in his hand.

"Here, take it. You've got an eye for talent, and I'm actually looking to hire a new girl. If you know someone you'd consider worthy of being a Nolan Knockout, give her my card and have her mention you. If she gets the job, I'll give you a referral bonus. Maybe even make you an extra in the newest commercial I'm—"

"Deal!" Jim said.

"Good man. Well look, it's ah," he looked at his Rolex and shook his head. "It's almost one o'clock, and I have to prepare a few things for a showing Ms. Scanlon is having here this afternoon. So if you'll excuse me, I'll give you a call after I talk to Bill at TBQ. It'll probably be sometime on Tuesday night or Wednesday. How's that sound?"

"That sounds great. Hey, thanks so much, Mr. Nolan."

"Forget it. I'll be in touch." Cal shook his hand and headed back to the house. Sarah was still looking at her phone as he passed by, and Cal wolf-whistled at her.

She snapped her head up.

"Have a good day, Hollywood," he said, heading inside the house as the door swung shut behind him. Jim danced in a circle and ran back to her before she could respond to Cal's taunt.

"There's my girl!" he said, kissing her cheek before she could pull away.

"Did you just hear that?" she asked.

"Meh, it wasn't even a good whistle. But check this out - he just told me he's going to get me a job at TBQ. Isn't that fantastic?" he asked while he danced around her.

"He's getting you a job?" she asked, frowning.

He stopped dancing when he saw her facial expression. "Oh god, now I have a chance at a sales job around here in software and you're still not happy. Do you realize how much money I could make there?"

"He hasn't even seen your resume. Doesn't that seem a bit too generous to you?"

"Maybe he just has an eye for talent."

"You don't just offer up something like that without a damn good reason. He must be up to something. Maybe he's trying to buy you off."

"Unbelievable," he said and threw up his hands. "Look, I know this guy gets under your skin, and I'll admit, he can be a bit of a prick. But I'm not passing up this job just because you've got some crazy hunch. I mean, just think what this could mean for us. Don't you want to retire before you're eighty?"

"Not if it means doing it with his help," she said. "I'm telling you—"

"You know what? Fine," he said and headed back towards the car. "Then I'm taking that job in Texas."

She caught up to him, stopping him and taking his hand. "No, Jimmy, I don't want you to do that either. I'd miss you."

He half-smiled and took her other hand. "I'd miss you too, but I never planned on staying in this job permanently. You know that."

"I know, but you're good at this and—"

"That's not the point," he said, tugging on her hands as he spoke. "This TBQ job could be my big chance, and I can't just dismiss it out of hand because you've got a hunch about Cal Nolan's motives." Sarah closed her eyes and looked at the ground as he spoke, appearing unmoved by his argument. He tilted her head back up towards him and smiled. "C'mon beautiful, if we want to ever get to this stupid wedding, we better get moving. You can be paranoid in the car while I'm figuring out where to build our retirement home." They walked to the car as he squeezed her hand.

"Okay," she said, "But I still want to—" Another car revved its engine as it came down the driveway. A blue Porsche pulled in behind Cal's car and came within inches of hitting its bumper.

"Guess Jane's here," he said, nodding at the new arrival.

"Miss Goo-Goo Eyes from yesterday?"

"That's the one."

Jane stepped out after she turned the engine off. She saw Jim and Sarah standing by their car and pointed towards the door.

"Is Mr. Nolan inside?" she asked, her long legs headed in that direction even before they could answer. "Oh, never mind, I see him through the window."

"Would you look at that outfit," Sarah said under her breath. "Fishnets, are you kidding me? But I do like her—" she stopped and started digging her long red nails into the back of his hand.

"Ahhhh!" he screamed and pulled his hand away in pain.

"Is everything alright?" Jane stopped and asked.

"Yeah, I'm fine, everything's great. Just a hand cramp," he said, holding his hand as Sarah regained her earlier scowl. Jane started to ask him something, but Cal tapped on the window and gestured for her to come inside.

"What the hell was that for?" Jim asked as they got in the car. "You're going to give me a scar like Jane's."

"Maybe if you weren't so distracted by her legs you'd—"

"It wasn't just her legs that distracted me."

"Oh, you're a riot. I can't believe you don't know why I'm upset."

He looked at his injured hand and eyed Sarah's legs. "Oh! Wait, why are you so upset about that?"

"Are you serious? Why didn't you tell me if you really thought I'd be happy you bought the exact same shoes you saw on her?"

"I don't know, maybe because you got all crazy thinking I saw Carol wearing them. Which I didn't, by the way."

"It doesn't matter who was wearing them! You only bought them because you got all Kit Katty seeing Jane in them."

"That's not—"

She put her hand up and turned away. "Just leave me alone."

They headed up the driveway and rode in silence for ten minutes. Each attempt Jim made to break the ice, Sarah rebuffed with either a sigh or an eye roll. He moved to use the hands-free phone, but pulled away when she slapped his hand.

"C'mon, this is silly," he said. "I need to call my office."

"Do it later," she said. "I don't want to hear your voice."

He scratched his forehead. "Is this how it's going to be the whole time we're at the wedding?"

"Maybe."

"I'm sorry, alright? I didn't get all Kit Katty or whatever seeing Jane in them."

"Uh huh, sure you didn't."

"Sarah, please don't be mad. I honestly am sorry. Did seeing them on Jane prompt me to buy them? Well yeah, but only because I thought you'd look way hotter in them than she did. I wasn't trying to hurt your feelings."

She took a deep breath but didn't respond.

"I love you?"

She glanced over at him and unfolded her arms. "Fine, call your office."

He breathed a sigh of relief. "Thank you," he said.

"Oh, I'm still mad at you. I just—"

"Love me too? I know." He punched a button in the center console to voice dial the dispatch office on speakerphone. "Call CRC Dispatch," he ordered the unit.

There was a momentary pause before the female voice on the speakerphone said, "Say a command."

"C'mon, Call CRC Dispatch," he asked again.

"Please try again," the voice prodded.

"Would you just call CRC Dispatch already?" he said.

"Did you say—Call CVS Pharmacy?"

"Dammit, this stupid piece of shit!"

"Sorry—no address book entry for Pizza Hut. Please try again."

As he smacked his hand on the steering wheel, Sarah calmly leaned forward.

"Call C-R-C Dis-patch," she enunciated carefully.

"Calling," the unit said. She leaned back in her seat and smirked.

"How did you -"

"Maybe you should be a little more patient with some things."

"CRC Dispatch, this is Catherine," the phone barked.

Just my luck, he thought. Catherine was a frumpy older woman a few years from retirement age. And while she was hardly a fan of Jim's, she thought the world of Sarah. Ever since Catherine had met her, he'd endured several "You better take care of that girl, she's too good for the likes of you" type comments whenever he worked with her.

"Hi Catherine, it's Jim Knox here."

"So?"

"I guess Lisa's not working today, huh."

"You leave that poor child alone."

"What? I just meant—"

"She's in Cancun for the week. A girl that pale is going to fry like a lobster down there."

"Really? She didn't mention it to me yesterday."

"Little Miss College thing needs to clear her schedule with you, does she, Jimmy?"

"No, I just thought since, you know, I was in and—"

"Maybe Lisa wasn't keen on letting Mr. Middle Age know where she'd be shaking her moneymaker for fall break."

Sarah covered her mouth but still laughed out loud. There were very few people who could out-snark Jim, but Catherine was one who always seemed to get the best of him.

"Sarah!" Catherine said excitedly. "Is that you, hon? How are you doing?"

"Hi Cathy, I'm just fine. How are you?"

"I'm good, I'm good. So what is your husband up to with Cal Nolan? I got some hussy from the CEO's office calling every two minutes looking to speak to that jackass Derek about something Jim was doing for him."

"That's right," Jim said. "I'm a superstar."

"You're a damn fool, that's what you are."

"Whatever, Catherine. Can you just tell Derek I installed a new splitter at the Exton house and I'll fax in a work order tomorrow?"

"What do I look like, your secretary?" she said. "Tell that jackass yourself."

"No, I don't—"

Sarah laughed as the hold music started playing over the speakerphone.

"What's the matter, Mr. Middle Age? Cathy got your tongue?" she asked.

"Shut up," he said.

Catherine returned to the line. "He's on the other line with someone talking about you superstar, so you'll have to call back later."

"Why can't he call me back?" he asked.

"You can ask that jackass when you call later. Goodbye Miss Sarah." She hung up as Sarah howled.

"Why do you encourage her?" he asked.

"I think it's important someone keeps you in line now and again," she said. "And I can't keep an eye on you 24-7."

The exit for the chapel appeared. He slowed down and took the next off-ramp, gripping and releasing the steering wheel as he tried to relax. "Well, you'll have to find a new partner in crime when I'm working at TBQ." He turned into the church parking lot and pulled into the first available spot.

"Jimmy, can we please talk more about that job when we get home. I'm still suspicious—"

"Of course." He sighed and wiped his hand across his face. "I'll tell you what. I'll listen to any kooky theories you have around Cal and that job later, but only if that gets me off the hook for the shoes. Agreed?"

She smiled and nodded. "Agreed. Now do something with your hair." She pulled a thin green hairbrush from her purse. "Here, use this."

"Kind of small, don't you think?" he asked. "Besides, I'm sure it's not that bad."

She took his chin and turned his head towards the rearview mirror. It was obvious he needed to do something with his hair.

"Give it here."

He grabbed it from her and tried combing his thick brown hair with it, but it wasn't the best tool for the job.

"How about now?"

They exited the car, and she walked over to inspect his handiwork.

"It looks like you spent ten seconds using my brush," she said

"Well, it'll have to do." He handed the comb back to her and adjusted his tie in the rearview mirror. "You ready to go in?" he asked, but she didn't respond. She was staring at her feet and tapping her teeth with her fingernails. "Sarah?"

"Hmm? Oh sorry, I was just putting together some things in my head."

"Jesus, you really are a Velma."

She laughed as they walked together towards the church entrance.

"Puzzles have always intrigued me, Jim. I'm still trying to figure you out, aren't I?"

5

They'd only been home from the wedding reception for thirty minutes, and Sarah was in full research mode as he'd gone into the bathroom to shower. She hadn't bothered changing clothes, so she could start work the moment they walked in. Her usual information gathering tools, including her notepads, multiple pens and their laptop were laid out across the bed. It'd been awhile since he'd seen her try to solve any sort of mystery, the last one being when he lost the remote control. She'd spent hours tracking it down only to discover he'd left it in the freezer while getting an ice cream sandwich. Jim heard the music blaring from the computer speakers as he put on his clothes.

"Can you turn that down please?" Jim asked, poking his head out of the bathroom. Steam poured out the door. "I'm trying to get dressed."

She looked up from the computer screen and took a sip of wine from the glass by the bed. "You're putting on a t-shirt and sweatpants. How distracting can it possibly be?"

"You try getting dressed while some guy keeps yelling 'Jam On It' at you."

"I'm not playing 'Jam On It.' It doesn't even sound like that stupid song."

"Oh. Are you playing 'Humpty Dance' then?"

"Would you quit stalling and get out here?"

Jim shut the door and turned the fan on to drown out the music as he finished toweling off. He weighed his chances of having sex with her tonight, and decided it was a longshot, but he'd use mouthwash anyway. He re-emerged and plopped down on the bed next to her.

"Alright, Jiggly-Puff," he said. "I'm ready. Do I get a tin foil hat to wear?"

"Only if you make it," she said. "But I did a little research and—"

He picked up the pad next to her and flipped through the pages.

"A little? You have three pages of notes here!"

"It's only two-and-a-half. And it's just an outline, it's no big deal."

"You used the standard Harvard format?"

"Well, that's what I always do for Mr. Donald, so I'm just used to doing it that way."

"Roman Numeral One, Introduction. Roman Numeral Two, Cal Nolan. Roman Numeral Three, My wife is insane."

"Give me that," she said and snapped the pad back from him. "Are you going to listen or make fun?"

"Probably a little from column A, and a little from column B."

"For now just listen. I think you're happier at CRC than you let on, but if you really want a job at TBQ, I want you to get it on your own, and not as some bribe from Cal Nolan. Why do you think he put all that effort in today? Because some things just don't add up for me."

"Since when does Shaggy have to start filling in the blanks? You're driving this van, Velma. I'm just riding back here with Phyllis Diller and the Globetrotters."

"First off, Fred always drives. Second, I'm not asking you to drive, I'm just looking for your take on what happened."

"Fine, Shaggy can do some spitballing," he said. "To answer your question, I'd guess the owner is either a friend or somebody important, and he wanted to make sure there were no hiccups."

"Okay, let's say that's the case. Did it seem like he was trying very hard to sell it?"

"Well, yeah, he took care of the cable thing for him, remember?"

"Forget the cable thing for a second. Why did he have the realty sign in the window of the house and not up at the road?"

"That's not unusual," he said. "People have realty signs in their window all the time."

"True, but you couldn't even see the house from the road. So if you drove by, how would you know it was for sale?"

"It was on a cul-de-sac. Nobody was just driving by there unless they had an appointment."

"Fair point. So schedule an appointment for me to view that house." She handed Jim the laptop and already had the browser window open to Nolan Realty's current listings. He took the laptop and clicked onto the list of realtors instead.

"Jim, c'mon, I had it open to where I wanted you to look."

"Do the homes have bikini shots too?" he asked.

"I'll get to the Knockouts in a minute, just look where I told you to."

"Fine." He clicked back and looked through the current homes available, both for rent and for sale and then tried a search for that particular address. "It's not on here," he said.

"No, it's not. I couldn't find that house listed anywhere, and the last sale date was seven years ago."

"Maybe it's a new listing, and it isn't going live on the website till Monday. Or maybe they're just managing the property for the guy while he's out of town, and he asked they sell it privately."

"The guy being Doug Flynn, right?"

"Well sure, isn't it?"

"I don't know, actually. The house was purchased under the name of a company. A company called BRM, LLC. The company isn't registered in Pennsylvania according to the state website, so I haven't found the owner yet."

"Okay, so, a company owns this house, not a person?"

She took a sip of her wine before answering. "Not exactly. You can set up something called a limited liability company to shield your identity in a sale if you don't want people seeing you bought a house. I've seen Mr. Donald do it for some of our customers. There are also certain tax benefits to doing it, but it's not something you see all that often."

"Well, then it makes even more sense they'd be selling it privately. Probably the owner is some fancy-pants and doesn't want the hoi polloi wandering around his house. Cal steps in when there's a problem with the cable because he's a big shot, and ta-da, mystery solved!"

"Hoi Polloi? Breaking out the big words tonight, are we?"

"What? It's my favorite *Three Stooges* episode. Now if you'll excuse me, Shaggy wants some peanut butter cup ice cream before he goes to bed unless we were going to, you know—" Jim walked his fingers along her leg.

"We weren't, and I'm not finished yet," she said, removing his hand. "You're ignoring Roman Numeral five." She pointed at the paper with her pen.

"Jane Scanlon? So what?"

"She's not on the website either, or anywhere else on the web for that matter. And yes, you can check for yourself," she said. He picked up the laptop and started clicking through the realtors. "Let's see, Alyssa, Amy, Andrea, Angela—"

"Alright, that's enough confirming," she said and reclaimed the laptop. "She doesn't appear to work for Nolan Realty, does she?"

"Not as a Knockout, anyway. Or maybe she's new and not on the website, either."

"So you think that's it? That all of this is just one happy coincidence and Cal Nolan puts his newest agent on a house so important that he personally shows up to fix a problem with the cable?"

"It's because she was new that he showed up, to give her every chance to succeed. That's the sign of a good manager."

"Baloney," she said. "It's the sign of a guy who's fooling around on his wife with a prostitute calling herself Jane Scanlon."

"You think she's a hooker?" He took the wine glass off the bedside table and drank the rest of it.

"Hey, I wasn't finished with that," she said.

"Oh, you've had plenty. There is no way she was a hooker."

"Think about it, Jim. Cal's got this unlisted house. It's out of the way. He can come and go as he pleases, and if anyone asks, either one of them just points to the sign in the window and says they're there for a house showing."

"Yeah, except you forgot something. Well you didn't forget, I just didn't mention it to you. The reason I knew her name was Jane was I heard her talking on the phone to someone and enunciating it. Then they put her on hold. You really think she's setting up anything under her hooker name that she has to call customer service for?"

Sarah looked at him for a moment, tapping her fingers on the computer. "You're sure?"

"Yes, I'm sure. So I doubt very much she's a hooker. In fact, I didn't get the impression they were sleeping together at all, hooker or no hooker."

"Please," she said. She set the laptop aside, jumped off the bed, and took off her pantyhose. "They're definitely sleeping together. I could tell that the moment you said her name to him."

"I don't doubt the guy might be nailing someone on the side, but there's no way you could tell it was Jane."

"That's because you can't read people like I can. It's why I always clean you and your friends out at poker." She hung up her dress in the closet.

"Oh really? What's my big tell then, Teddy KGB?"

"Every time you bluff, you scratch the back of your neck," she said as she pulled on a green t-shirt.

"Is that so? Then why can't you tell when I'm bluffing whenever we're bridge partners?"

"Because you aren't supposed to bluff your partner in bridge."

"You aren't?"

"No!"

"Oh," he said. "Then let's say you're right. Does that mean you're fine with me accepting the help of a regular adulterer, just not a john?"

"I'm not fine with you accepting the help of Cal Nolan, period," she said. She finished putting on her woolly pajama bottoms and walked into the bathroom. "It doesn't matter which one he is, if he's cheating on his wife, he's going to get burned. He loses everything in the divorce if he's caught. Why would anyone risk that?"

"You did actually see Jane today, didn't you?"

She rolled her eyes and shut the door. He propped up some pillows on the bed and grabbed her notepad. The notes she'd taken were well-written in cursive, and had extensive citations referring to the sources for each item. *It's no wonder Mr. Donald won't share her*, he thought.

"So would you throw it all away to be with someone like Jane?" she asked as she came out of the bathroom and climbed into bed next to him.

"Nope," he said without looking up. "Too much paperwork."

"And grandmother thought you weren't a catch."

"No, she just thought I was a heathen."

"She never actually called you a heathen," she said.

"Look, let's not quibble over some every small detail."

"That's a small detail?"

"It's neither here nor there," he said. "Hey, did you see the guy at table seven that looked like my grandfather?"

"Yes!" she said, putting her hand on him. "The resemblance was eerie. It was like he'd come back from the dead or something."

He sighed. "I just wish you could have met him back when my grandmother was alive. She was the best. I'll never forget the last story time we had together."

"Why, what happened?"

"Well, I guess I was six when she came over that last time to visit. I kind of knew she was sick, but I didn't know how bad it was. So when we did story time the last night she was there, my dad taped it with his old Super 8 video camera. She said she wanted to read all my favorites, so she spent over an hour reading my favorite books. We acted out *Caps for Sale*, *Frog and Toad Are Friends* and *Where the Wild Things Are*. Then after she passed away, my dad set up the projector every year, and I'd watch her reading to me just like she did that night. There was no sound with Super 8 tapes, but I knew every word by heart and heard my grandmother's voice saying them just the same." He took a deep breath and covered his face.

"Oh Jimmy," she said, caressing his back. "That's one of the sweetest stories I've ever heard."

"Yeah," he said, "I thought so too when I saw it on the Hallmark channel last month."

"What?"

"Ha, ha, gotcha!" he said. "Tee hee! Guess you can't read me quite so well after all."

"I'm going to kill you," she said. She pummeled him with her pillow while he covered his face and laughed hysterically.

"Stop, stop, I'm sorry," he said, "But this Cal the criminal nonsense is just as silly. There's nothing to your theory, and his only 'crimes' seem to be he's horny and loves baked goods, unless I missed something in Roman Numeral six, section B."

"I only had half an hour, and I was rushing. If I had time to do a full investigation—"

"A full investigation?" he asked, rolling off the bed onto his feet. "Tell you what, Velma. No matter how much you dig, you won't find Cal's done anything illegal. Because the only way I'm passing up an opportunity like this is if he's an honest to goodness crook."

"No, no bets," she said, waving him off. "I'm not going through that nonsense I did with Chick-Fil-A." Their last bet had centered on whether he could go without ice cream for a month. She found him one day eating a cup of it from Chick-Fil-A in the living room. He argued for hours it was not really "ice cream" because they called it "Ice Dream," and she was forced to finally concede the point when he called the corporate office and had them tell her it couldn't technically be considered "ice cream" because there was no cream in it.

"It's not really a bet, per se. More of a challenge from someone who doesn't think you're quite the sleuth you think you are. And I figure this is the only way I can take another sales job without you nagging me for the next ten years about it."

"I'm an excellent sleuth, but I don't really have time—"

He began playing a mock violin. "Boo hoo hoo. You're just making excuses because I was right, and you were wrong. If you really thought you could discover Cal was haunting an old amusement park, you'd have no problem finding the time." He stopped to turn off the light as he headed downstairs. "Sweet dreams, Hollywood."

"Fine!" She jumped out of bed and grabbed his shirt before he could leave. "What do I have to do?"

"You have two days to dig around," he said. "If you find proof by midnight on Tuesday that he's some sort of master criminal and wasn't just someone you found irritating, I won't do the deal, and I'll never mention Texas again. But if you can't, you have to promise to drop the whole thing and support my decision to take whatever job I want."

"Two days? That's it?"

"Two days for you is like a month for a normal person. If you can't do it in two days, there's nothing there."

She nodded. "Alright, you're on." They shook hands as she flashed a smug smile.

"Now give me some sugar baby," Jim said, and tried to pull her into his arms.

Sarah pushed him off of her and through the open doorway. "Sorry, Sugar Daddy. I've got work to do." She closed the door in his face.

6

Sarah arrived at her desk shortly before 8:00 a.m. on Monday morning. The crisp fall walk from the train station downtown to her office was a short one, so the entire trip only took about forty minutes to complete. Normally Jim dropped her at the station if he was working, but since he wasn't scheduled today, that was a lost cause from the moment she tried shaking him to get up. When all she got in response was a muffled groan and what sounded like, "Hit by a taxi," she gave up and drove herself to the station, but not without first strategically taping Jim's unfinished shopping list on the TV.

She hung up her maroon suit jacket, slid into her chair and set her bag on the floor. Her yellow notepad peeked out of the front pocket. The three pages of notes she'd taken last night had grown to six, but she wasn't any closer to proving anything than when she started.

Mr. Donald, tipping his hat as he walked by her desk and into his office, said "Good morning, Mrs. Knox." He wore his usual attire, which was a plaid, light blue three-piece suit and matching striped tie. He was seventy-five-years-old, but thanks in no small part to Sarah's efficiency, he showed no signs of slowing down.

"Good morning, Mr. Donald," she said and turned on her PC. She waited until he was settled before she took a notebook from her desk drawer and printed out his schedule for the day. She walked into his office and sat down in one of the red leather chairs in front of his desk. There were a few pictures of him with his sister on the wall along with a copy of his honorable discharge from the army, dated 1954.

"Have you seen that notebook I had?" he asked while searching through his desk drawers.

"Which one is that, Mr. Donald? I've got them organized for you based on color and date."

"Oh, it's the last one I used, I think," he said

"That's over my by desk." She pointed back to her desk, and he leaned over to get a better look.

"Yes, that's it. Would you mind getting it for me?"

She walked back out into the hallway and retrieved the notepad for him. It was jammed with handwritten notes he'd made and she'd organized by using a series of endnotes and printing a short bibliography that she'd slipped in the back. The office communication methods he used were straight from the 1970s. He didn't use e-mail for anything except what she typed up on his behalf, and he asked her to print out anything urgent he should see. He had an assigned Blackberry, which never left her desk, and he liked to issue paper memos for employee mailboxes.

"Here you go, Mr. Donald, and here's your schedule."

"Thank you."

"You have a 9:00 a.m. appointment with Mr. Milligan at his office, and then you've got a doctor's appointment scheduled at 10:30. You asked me last week to keep your afternoon open today, so perhaps we can spend some time then going over some of those PowerPoint slides I've put together for your meeting on Wednesday morning?"

"Actually, Mrs. Knox, I asked you to keep my schedule open in case I need to be out of the office this afternoon, and I do," he said. "The tests I've scheduled are apparently quite tiring, so the doctor asked I rest for a few hours once they're completed. Can you schedule a car to pick me up at Philadelphia Hospital around 12:30?"

"Yes, yes, of course," she said, jotting down some notes. "Is everything alright? What kind of car would you like? Last time I believe we used a—"

"I'm fine, and any car you come up with is fine." Despite his assurances, she was still concerned. He'd scheduled this appointment on his own a few weeks ago and hadn't told her what it was for. "That's enough about all that," he said, slapping his hand on the desk and smiling. "I'm sure you'll manage in my absence, since you and I both know you're the brains behind this operation."

"That's not true, but that's very nice of you to say, thank you." She smiled and turned to leave. "Is there anything else you might like me to do while you're out today? I could take some time to write thank you notes for some of the clients we've already filed tax returns for this year."

"No, that's quite alright. Mr. Kim's office did request your help with the Nolan Realty—"

"I could help with that," she said, trying not to sound too anxious.

"Nonsense," he said. "I already told him we're spending too much time dealing with this during tax season."

"I don't mind, really. Rory told me last week he needed a hand, so I'd be glad to help out."

"Very well. I just hate the idea of wasting your talents on anything involving Calvin."

"Mr. Donald, do you mind if I ask why you hate him so much?"

He shook his head. "He's taken his father's company and turned it into this burlesque show in order to line his already bulging pockets. Irvin never cared about anything other than helping his customers. Cal only seems to care about helping himself."

"So all his charity work—"

"Is a tax strategy devised by Mr. Kim. Although I'll admit, that sandwich bearing his name is quite delicious." They both laughed. "Does that answer your question?"

"Yes, thank you," she said. "I won't let it interfere with my regular duties, I promise."

"I know it won't. Let's see," he said as he got up and checked his silver pocket watch, "I think I'll head out now and grab something to eat before that meeting at nine. I'll see you tomorrow, Mrs. Knox."

"Goodbye, Mr. Donald. And don't forget we're doing story time down at the library tomorrow morning." A city-wide day of community service for Philadelphia businesses was scheduled for tomorrow, and he'd volunteered himself and Sarah to read at one of the libraries in danger of being shut down.

He smiled. "I'm looking forward to it. I'll see you in the morning." He picked up his coat and hat and headed past her towards the elevators.

Returning to her desk, she logged back in and stretched before calling Rory Bauer from Mr. Kim's office. Rory was Mr. Kim's executive assistant and her closest friend at the company.

"Hi Sarah," he said. "Is Mr. Donald in yet?"

"He left for the day, actually," she said. "That's why I was calling."

"You want to get some coffee?" he asked. "I can walk down with you."

"Sure, we can do that. But I was wondering if you started gathering that stuff for the Nolan case?"

"Not yet," he said. "I've been putting it off as long as possible."

"Well," she said, twirling the phone cord as she spoke, "I thought since Mr. Donald was gone for the day I could give you a hand. Maybe organize things a bit for you."

"Don't toy with me, Sarah."

"I wouldn't do that. You want me to call down to Gary in IT to print out all the e-mail correspondence from the last year?"

"Yes!" he said. "I was dreading having to talk to that sourpuss. Thank you."

"Let me call there now. I'll walk over to you when I'm done."

"Sounds good. And thanks again, really."

"Just glad I can help."

She smiled and sat on her desk corner as she called into the hold queue for the support desk, drumming her fingers and waiting for someone to save her from listening to the same dreadful cover of AC/DC's "Moneytalks."

"IT Support, this is Gary."

She could hear him yawning through the phone. "Hey, Gary, it's Sarah Knox, from Mr. Donald's office? How are you today?"

"Peachy. What can I do for you, Mrs. Knox?"

"Can you give me access to the e-mail archive administrative console? I want to start printing out and organizing our communications for the Nolan Realty case."

"Sure, that's fine. Actually, if you want, I could just dump all the Nolan Realty e-mails into a big spreadsheet or something," he said although she thought she could hear him physically biting his tongue as he finished speaking.

"That would be helpful, thank you. I'd like to have both options, and could you make sure the spreadsheet's separated out into different tabs? It needs to be sorted based on title, subject, date, sender, recipients, and miscellaneous keywords."

"Boy, sorry I asked," he mumbled.

"Excuse me?"

"Nothing, I'll take care of it. I just activated your login ID/ password. The system generated note should be sent via e-mail in a minute or so."

She stayed on the line and waited only moments before the e-mail appeared in her inbox. She logged in and moved the keyboard onto her lap.

"Yep, I'm in," she said.

"Oh boy," he said and hung up on her. She picked up the receiver to call back but shook her head and placed the phone back in the cradle to work on more pressing business.

She typed "Jane Scanlon" into the search area. No results found, the system told her. She cleared the entry area and typed "Doug Flynn." Same result.

An instant message from Jim popped on her screen. *Good, he's at least up*, she thought.

ClubberLangIsAwesome: Hi Velma. Have you seen Scrappy-Doo?

SarahKnoxInPhilly: Very funny.

Jim had multiple screen names, and he kept adding new ones to gauge her reaction and see just how "clever" it was. This particular one used to be his main IM and e-mail address, but once she pointed out how dumb it looked on the top of his resume, he switched to a more professional address.

ClubberLangIsAwesome: Just kidding.

SarahKnoxInPhilly: Are we still on for lunch?

ClubberLangIsAwesome: Yes. What time?

SarahKnoxInPhilly: 12:30

ClubberLangIsAwesome: cool I'm in the mood for tex-mex.

SarahKnoxInPhilly: Knock it off.

ClubberLangIsAwesome: teehee. whatcha doin

SarahKnoxInPhilly: I'm looking through old e-mails from Nolan Realty.

ClubberLangIsAwesome: of course you are. my crazy wife

SarahKnoxInPhilly: ☺. What are you doing?

ClubberLangIsAwesome: looking at tuxedos
SarahKnoxInPhilly: Jimmy
ClubberLangIsAwesome: LOL
SarahKnoxInPhilly: Meet me in lobby at 12:30. Ok?
ClubberLangIsAwesome: will do. bye daphne
SarahKnoxInPhilly: velma!

She closed the chat window to resume her work, and typed 714 Timothy Court into the search engine. A new window popped up with a single result, showing one e-mail and its contents—

From: Brown, Rachel [rbrown@nolanrealty.com]
Sent: Thursday, September 7, 4:57 PM
To: Dever, Rita [rita.dever@donaldandkim.com]
Subject: Sorry
Importance: Normal

Hey Rita,

Sorry I didn't get back to you sooner. I just spoke to Mr. Nolan, and there aren't any positions opening up for a few months. I'm sorry you hate it there so much, and I'll let you know when something opens up.

Anyway, can you do me a favor? I screwed up and accidentally sent you the following invoice before I should have -

Invoice 4501050328/09 for 1425 Spruce Street, Philadelphia, PA

We were late getting the rent from Myrtle in office 4B again, but she finally paid up, and I need to adjust the invoice amount accordingly. Boy does that woman hate Mr. Nolan.

I'll let you know when the lease is up on that condo in Malvern you wanted, although I'm guessing it won't be until January. There's a house in Exton on 714 Timothy Court that sounds like it might be available for rent soon, but not exactly sure when. I overheard Mr. Nolan telling someone to meet him out there for a walkthrough. Let me see if I can find out more about it.

See you at happy hour at B&F's tomorrow!

Rachel Brown
Office Administrator
Nolan Realty, Inc.
1249 Chestnut Street
(215)555-4263 - Phone
(215)555-4264—Fax

Sarah knew if Mr. Donald saw this e-mail he wouldn't be pleased. She'd only met Rita once since she'd been hired five months ago and was surprised she'd be looking to get out so soon after landing the job. Rita's extension rang twice before she answered.

"Accounts Payable, this is Rita."

"Hey Rita, this is Sarah Knox from Mr. Donald's office."

"Hi, Sarah. What I can do for you?"

"I'm pulling together some archived e-mails for the partners, and I'd like to discuss one that Rachel Brown sent to you last month. The one from September seventh, specifically."

"September seventh?" Rita asked. "I'm sorry Sarah, I'm not sure which e-mail you're referring to."

"Well, you seem to be looking for other employment in the one I have."

The line was silent for a few moments.

"Rita?" she asked.

"Oh God, I forgot all about that. I'm fired, aren't I?"

"I didn't say that. I just want—"

"Please Sarah, I'm so sorry. I was just having a rough week last month, I don't want to leave. I was mad and venting to Rachel, and she sent that e-mail and—"

"Rita, calm down. I just want to ask you about it, that's all. Did you ever hear if that house in Exton that Rachel mentioned became available for rent?"

"No, it never did," she said. "Mr. Nolan told her the owner decided to have some work done, and it wouldn't be available for several more weeks."

"Is that so?" she asked as she got her pad and took down some notes. "Did she say why he was doing a walkthrough then?"

"She said it was a misunderstanding, and he just meant he was seeing how the work on the place was going."

"Did she mention what was being done?"

"I think she said it was remodeling? I'm not sure, I could check with her if you wanted."

"Actually, if you don't mind . . ."

"Please, no, whatever you need. I can call her right now."

"Anytime is fine as long as it's before 11:30. Oh, one last thing—what was this invoice she asked to pull?"

"That was nothing. Nolan Realty leases a building near the hospital and apparently this one tenant is upset about the office she's in and keeps fighting with them about the rent. I just needed to adjust the invoice once she sent in her rent payment. That's all."

"I see," Sarah said. "Would you happen to have any information around the building and the various tenants you could send up to me? I'm working on getting together some material for that lawsuit, and I'd like to have it for the files we're preparing."

"Absolutely, I'll take care of it. Is there anything else I can do?"

"No, I think that's all. I'll look forward to hearing from you."

"I'll get back to you about both items sometime this morning," Rita said. "Thank you so much, Sarah."

"Sure thing. Bye Rita." She hung up the phone and put down her pen to print out the e-mail. After she printed it, she tucked it in her purse and reset her search to get everything over the past year. As the printer roared to life, she grabbed her wallet to get her coffee.

Rory was on the phone when she arrived at his cubicle. He gestured he'd be another minute, so she leaned against the wall and checked Jim's Facebook status from her phone. "Jim Knox is having lunch with a knockout today," it read. She smiled as Rory finished the call and sidled up to her.

"Let's go," he said. They headed into the stairwell by Mr. Kim's office to go down to the lobby.

"I'm printing out all those e-mails now," she said. "I'll start organizing them when I get back."

"Thank god. Mr. Kim wants to give everything to the lawyers soon and be done with it."

"When are we turning this stuff over?"

"Search me. Judge Snyder hasn't said boo about anything these last few months."

"I know, but since Beth did that interview on Saturday, I thought he'd be back at it. He seems to follow her lead on everything, so if she's out and about, figured he'd be as well," she said, opening the door to the lobby. The coffee cart had a line of people waiting, which wasn't unusual for a Monday morning. "There's really nothing going on in that case still?"

"No, although I heard some of the plaintiffs are grumbling it's going so slowly," Rory said. "You'd think they'd be a little more patient with the judge. He's the only chance they have, and he's been through a lot."

"I'd be frustrated too if I'd been waiting a year since some bimbo replaced me. But I doubt they're actually blaming the judge. I'm sure it's Cal Nolan's fault it's dragging out so long."

"Probably, but they knew what they were getting into. You can't take a guy like Cal Nolan on and expect results overnight."

"Can I take your order?" the young male barista asked.

"Oh, I'll have a tall regular coffee," he said, "And whatever she wants. I've got both." He placed a ten dollar bill on the counter.

"I'll have a tall non-fat mocha, but please make sure you use the organic chocolate," she said. She watched the barista throughout the order to make sure he followed her instructions. She was satisfied he had, and they took their drinks off the countertop and headed back into the staircase.

"Thanks, Rory."

"Forget it. I owe you a lot more than a coffee." He sipped his coffee and grinned. "Mmm, delicioso," he said. "This is probably all just a waste of time. Maybe the judge will throw the case out just to spend more time with his granddaughter."

"God I hope not," she said.

"Shh, don't say that too loud," he said as he looked around and lowered his voice. "I thought I remembered you wanted Nolan to lose this case. Why did you suddenly offer to help me?"

"I'm just helping organize the evidence for a friend," she said. "If Cal's done something wrong, I'm sure he'll get what he deserves." She winked and headed back to her desk.

At 12:30, she found Jim waiting in the lobby entrance, which was a pleasant surprise since he was often late for lunch dates. They decided to go to Bartlett s Café, which was about a block and a half from her office and was one of her favorite spots to get lunch in the city. The tables and booths were cramped but cozy, and the small counter had five red stools. It was always crowded for lunch but appeared to be clearing out as they approached the host stand.

"Hi, how many?" asked the host as they walked up together.

"Seventeen," Jim said.

"Two, please," Sarah said, giving Jim a look. "We were hoping for a booth by the window, but it looks like you're full up."

"It'll be about twenty minutes for a booth. If you want to sit right away, the counter's free."

The counter was empty, so they accepted the offer. She sat down at the stool on the far end as Jim sat to her left and spun around a few times. He stopped when the waitress came over and poured them each a glass of water. She was an older woman with black hair poking out from a small white hat.

"Hi, folks. Welcome to Bartlett's. I'm Jody, and I'll be serving you today," Jody said.

"Hi Jody. My name's Sarah, and this is my husband Jim."

Jim shook his head as he watched this play out. Sarah knew it drove him nuts when she engaged the wait staff in idle chit-chat.

"Well, it's nice to meet you, Sarah. And Jim," Jody said. "Here are some menus, and I'll be right back to take your order."

"Why do you do that?" he asked. "It's so stupid."

"It isn't stupid. When I was a waitress—"

"Never mind," he said. "Do what you want."

"You don't have to be so grumpy about it."

"I'm sorry," he said, picking up his spoon and smacking it in his hand. "I'm annoyed at Derek, that's all. Although that's kind of a good news, bad news thing."

"What? Why?"

"Oh, he called all pissed off I went over his head about that house, and we got into a whole argument about it so he took me off the schedule. I called HR to explain what happened, and they told him he has to put me back on the schedule or he'll be suspended. So, the bad news is, I have twelve hour shifts on Thursday and Friday, and I'm on beeper all weekend for emergencies."

"You're not going to miss date night on Friday, are you?"

"No way, it's my turn to pick the movie. I'll be done by eight," he said, flipping the spoon in the air.

"Well that is good news," she said, catching the spoon and setting it back on the counter.

"It is, but that's not what I meant. He told them he wasn't going to work with a coddled superstar, so he requested a transfer."

She smiled and put her hand on his knee. "That's even better news. So maybe you'd consider staying now? Or maybe you could apply for Derek's job?"

"No, I wouldn't, and he's probably not going anywhere for awhile anyway. You need at least ten years of experience in a field office to even apply, so unless they have someone in mind, I doubt he'll be leaving anytime soon."

"Oh," she said, removing her hand. "Well, at least he's transferring at some point."

"Yeah, I guess," Jim said. "And you know why he asked me to take such drastic action in the first place? His sister was fired by Nolan Realty, so he was pissed this Flynn guy used them to sell his house."

"Too bad it's not actually for sale."

"Yeah, well, not publically anyway."

She shook her head. "It isn't for sale at all, Jim. It's a rental that isn't currently listed and hasn't been for months. Supposedly the owner is having some remodeling work done."

Jody approached and pulled a pad and pen out of her apron. "You folks decided yet?"

"Can I have an egg-white omelet with peppers, tomatoes, and onions along with some rye toast? And a cup of V8, please," Sarah said.

"Sure thing, Sarah. And for you, Jim?"

"I'll have the Heartattacker and a bottle of birch beer." Sarah looked at her menu to see the sandwich he ordered consisted of Italian sausage, American Cheese, fried onions and Russian dressing on a kaiser roll.

"Birch beer?" Sarah asked as they handed their menus back.

"Yeah, wanted to spice things up a bit," he said.

"Hey Doc, somebody actually ordered that crazy sandwich you like," Jody yelled. One of the short order cooks just waved at her and smiled. "Doc's my husband. Been working here thirty-seven years together."

"That's wonderful you've been married for so long," Sarah said.

Jody threw her head back and let out a belly laugh. "Married for thirty-seven years? Hell no! We've only been married for the last eleven. I couldn't have lived with that old fool for all thirty-seven years. Working together was plenty, but when I got divorced and Doc's wife died, well, we figured we could save on gas. Ain't that right, Doc?"

Doc waved her off again.

"My soulmate," she said. "Let me go put those in for you and get your drinks." She scribbled down her order on a pad and took it to the kitchen.

Jim waited for her to leave before turning back to Sarah. "Okay, so you're saying Nolan is the property manager for this house?"

"Yep. Here, let me show you," she said, pulling the e-mail she'd printed out of her purse. There were handwritten notes on every part of the page.

"Are you doing any actual work today?" he asked as she showed it to him.

"I'm ahead of schedule, actually. Mr. Donald had—"

"Here are your drinks," Jody said. "You folks holler if you need anything. I'll be back when Doc has finished up your orders."

Jim watched Jody walk off and asked, "Does she remind you of my Aunt Kate?"

"Not really. Now Myrtle there," she said, pointing to Myrtle's name in the printed e-mail. "She's like your Aunt Kate."

"Myrtle?" He took the note to see where she pointed. "How the hell would you know that? You never actually—oh god, you called her, didn't you?"

She nodded and picked some fuzz off his shirt sleeve. "Of course. A good detective follows up on every potential lead, and I'm always happy to talk to someone who hates Cal. I'm glad I did too because Myrtle is a hoot. She had me in stitches."

"Yeah, I'm sure she's a riot. You thought that crazy guy at the post office who called himself The Duke of Delivery was funny too."

"Oh speaking of, do you mind dropping this off later?" She reached over and took a small, bulging envelope out of her purse and handed it to him.

"What's in here?" he asked, shaking the envelope around. "Some 'We Hate Cal' Kool-Aid mix?"

"No, it's a 'The New Hollywood' supporter button."

"Well that's pretty random. What would she want their stupid button for?"

"It's not random. She collects buttons and didn't have this one."

"Gee I wonder why. Didn't she have time to grab the swag bag from the after-party before she and P-Diddy had to split?"

"Very funny," Sarah said.

"I know," he said. "If her name's Myrtle, she's gotta be a hundred years old, so she'd probably go with Englebert Humperdinck or something. Why don't you just mail that thing from your mailroom?"

"I was going to, but it's not enough postage, and since it's not a business—"

"Yeah, yeah, yeah, I got it. Whatever, I'll mail it to Lady Buttons. I got nothing else going on."

"Thank you," she said, leaning over to kiss him on the cheek. "And she really was pretty funny. She told me a joke you might like."

"I doubt it," Jim said, and stuck the envelope in his coat pocket. "But fire away."

"A dyslexic guy walks into a bra. Get it?"

"So he was a cross-dresser?"

Sarah rolled her eyes as Jody came back with their food. "Alright, enjoy your lunch and throw something at Doc if the food stinks. If you need anything, just holler." She patted the counter and left the check in front of them before heading behind the cash register to ring people up.

"How's that sandwich?" she asked, sipping her tomato juice.

He gave a thumbs-up as he chewed.

"Can you eat and listen to what else I found in my investigation?"

He swallowed and put the sandwich down to wipe his hands. "Go nuts. Perhaps you could start by explaining how you got access to this e-mail in the first place?" he asked. "Because I don't remember that being part of your day to day activities as Mr. Donald's assistant."

"I volunteered to help Rory gather up documents for the lawsuit against Nolan Realty. And of course a big part of that is making sure all the e-mail communication is accounted for."

"Volunteered huh? I should have known you'd have a few tricks up your sleeve."

"Of course," she said. "I had this girl Rita check on the status of the house. She called me back after she found out it hadn't been on the market for over a year, supposedly because the owner was doing work on the place. So there haven't been any showings, yesterday or any other day."

"A full year? Then why did—hmmm."

"Hmm what?" she asked.

"I'm just wondering why they kept the guy's cable turned on. I mean, you can suspend your service for up to a year. Just seems like a waste of money if no one's renting the place."

"That's what I thought. But what if someone was renting it off the books? Say, a Miss Jane Scanlon?"

"You think he stashed some mistress there for a full year?"

"Sure. That way his wife doesn't find out about it, and as long as the owner is getting paid a monthly check from Nolan Realty, he's not going to care."

Jim took another bite of his sandwich and chewed it slowly as he looked at the e-mail.

"C'mon Jim, admit it, I'm on to something."

He wiped his mouth with his sleeve and shook his head. "I'll admit he's probably sleeping with Jane. And perhaps she's even living there. But he hasn't committed a crime, has he?"

"No, but he's obviously—"

"If I turned down every job because some board member was having an affair, I'd be permanently unemployed. How do you even know it isn't this Flynn guy who's having the affair with her?"

"Because he's a happily married banker who lives in Kentucky."

"Kentucky?"

"Yeah, I finally found out where that BRM company was registered, and it's to a Doug Flynn in Kentucky. Including that house, he owns investment properties in seven states."

"What the hell does a Kentucky banker want with a house in Exton?"

"Well I spoke to his assistant for almost twenty minutes. She was so sweet, and believe it or not, he's a former baseball player for the Mets—"

"Boo!" he said, cupping his hands together.

"What was that for?" she asked.

"You just said the Mets, right?"

"Yeah, he—"

"Boo!"

She whacked him playfully on the arm. "Would you stop that? He doesn't play for them anymore."

"He's still tainted," he said "Perhaps I'll call Mr. Met myself and say hello. What's his phone number?"

"I'm not telling you that."

"Fine, but I'm just going to look it up online when I get home. You know how much I hate the Mets."

"Don't you dare," she warned him as she folded back up the paper. "He sounds like a wonderful person. Most of the money he makes from those properties is divvied up and donated to churches and charitable organizations."

"I don't believe it. It must be a trick or something."

"It's not a trick! Anyways, she told me his corporation was named after his first team, the Cincinnati Reds."

"BRM?" He thought for a moment and snapped his fingers. "Big Red Machine!" he said, referring to the nickname of the Reds teams in the 1970s. "You know who the Big Red Machine was?" he asked.

"Of course, Jim. My dad grew up loving Pete Rose."

"That's about right," he said as he finished his sandwich.

"What does that mean, exactly?"

"It uh, it means your dad loved someone who worked hard at his job every single day and never took a play off."

"Nice save."

He took a bow in his seat. "Thank you. So, what, now you go to Mrs. Nolan with your suspicions and leave Cal penniless?"

"Absolutely not," she said. "That's between him, his conscience and his wife. The point of this little exercise is not about me getting revenge."

"No, it's to make sure I stay in the same crappy job my entire life."

"That's not true, and you know it."

"Do I?" he asked.

She grimaced and looked back at him. "Jimmy, we had a—"

He put his hands up and nodded. "You're right, I'll stop."

"As I was saying, the agreement was I'd find proof he'd committed a crime by Tuesday at midnight. And adultery isn't a crime. It's like Samuel Johnson once said, 'Revenge is an act of passion; vengeance of justice. Injuries are revenged; crimes are avenged.'"

"Who in the hell is Samuel Johnson?" he asked.

"He was an English author in the 1700s," she said as he stared blankly at her. "I was an English Lit. major, remember?"

"Well then," he said as he picked up the check, "To quote American beatnik Norville Rogers, 'Like, let's get outta here!'" He grinned and walked over to the short line at the register to pay. Sarah pulled out her phone to Google Norville Rogers but was interrupted by an incoming call.

"Sarah Knox," she answered. Jim returned to drop the tip on the counter and sat back on his stool, watching her tug at her lip.

"Who is it?" he mouthed.

She got up from her stool and gathered her purse. "No, I understand. Are you sure everything is okay?" she asked. "Alright, give me about forty-five minutes, and I'll be over. Thank you." She sighed and put the phone back in her pocket.

"What's the matter?" he asked.

"Mr. Donald went in for some tests this morning and needs to be admitted until Thursday," she said. "He asked me to bring some things from his office and spend some time with him reviewing his schedule for the next few days."

"Is he okay?"

"He assured me he's fine, and it's something very minor. Look, I have to run back to the office. Can you give me a ride over to the hospital?"

"Of course," he said as he gave his hand to help her down from the stool. Sarah dropped some money in a donation jar for the Michele Groves foundation at the register as Jim scooped some mints into his hand. "All set," he said. "You want a mint?"

"I'll pass," she said. "Where are you parked?"

"It's actually the other direction from your office. How about I pick you up in front of your building in fifteen minutes? Or do you need me to help carry stuff down?"

She shook her head. "I think I can manage. So I'll meet you out front at 1:26?"

He laughed as he checked his watch. "That's fine. I can even do 1:27, but I've got a conflict at 1:28."

She pulled the door open and held it for him.

"Wait, what are you doing?" Jim asked. "This is my favorite part."

"I know, but you made fun."

"No, no, I was just kidding. Please?"

"Alright." She smiled and let him hold the door open for her, waving to Jody as she headed out.

7

"Going my way?" Jim asked, swinging the door to his van open for her. She set the file folder she'd put together for Mr. Donald on her seat, and he took her arm to help her in. He'd quickly cleaned the front area of the van and broken open a new air freshener with a picture of a pineapple wearing sunglasses. "This should be an interesting drive with the van since the side streets to get over there are awful."

"When were you there before?" she asked.

"My sister spent a week down there after falling out of a window at her friend's house when I was fourteen. I hope there's more parking available than there used to be. You basically couldn't get a spot near the hospital after nine in the morning. We parked every day in the same cheap garage over half mile away on Spruce and had to walk."

Traffic was heavy as they turned onto Walnut Street and headed west to the hospital. He attempted a shortcut that took them down a one way street, only to end up blocked behind a truck unloading beer at a local market. Sarah sighed and pulled out a pad and started making notes. Bored, he hit the voice dial button on his van's speakerphone.

"Call Token," he said, smiling when the unit affirmed his command. Sarah gave him a look and shifted away from Jim in her seat.

Token was the nickname his friends had long ago affixed to Eric Dawkins, the only member of his circle of friends that was black. It was neither clever nor unique, but that wasn't really their forte when it came to assigning nicknames. His hairy friend was called Yeti, their friend who drank a lot called Rummy, their Italian friend called Dego, etc. He hated his nickname Cheatmissioner, which grew out of a grossly unfair reading of a situation between him and Eric in fantasy football several years prior.

"This is Eric Dawkins."

Sarah sighed and flipped to a new page in her notebook.

"Token, what's up dude?" he asked.

"What's up, Mister Cheatmissioner?"

"Would you please stop calling me that?"

"Stop calling you Cheatmissioner? Fine, how about Cheatissioner? That's probably more grammatically correct anyways."

"No matter how you pronounce it, it's not true. I didn't cheat you."

"Oh, didn't you? Do you really want to argue that with the only barrister you know?"

"Quit calling yourself barrister. It sounds so stupid."

"It's better than calling myself Cheatmissioner."

"I don't call myself that!"

"You should, because you are, and you did."

"Nothing I did was illegal."

"But was it moral?"

"ESPN.com doesn't have a section in the fantasy football rules about what's moral."

"They should for cheaters like you."

"Look, it was your stupid trade proposal. All I did was accept."

"Beep, boop, beep, beep, boop."

"What are you doing?"

"Pushing your buttons," Eric said. "And right now I'm playing you like a Simon! Where are you at dude?"

"I just finished lunch with Sarah down at Bartlett's and now I'm dropping her—"

"No shit! I've been to that place. Did you see that weirdo behind the counter?"

"Yeah, we got stuck sitting there."

"I was there last week with some of the partners, and the whole place is shouting out answers and cheering for someone on *The Price is Right*. It was like eating at the diner from *Cop Rock* or something."

"*Cop Rock*!" Jim said. "Ha, that's awesome. Did you have to sing for your order?""

"Give me that whole Egg-White Omelet. Give me that whole Egg-White Omelet," Eric sang in a low baritone voice to the tune of "Give me that Old Time Religion." Jim laughed, and even Sarah chuckled as he sang.

"You two must be the only guys who still remember *Cop Rock* was even on TV," she said.

"My parents didn't have cable," Eric said.

"I just liked watching singing cops," Jim said. "Hey, are we still on for Saturday?"

"You bet, dude. What time should Yeti and I get over there?"

"Well, the convention doesn't start until ten, but I was hoping to get there early to make sure we can buy those comics from—"

"Comics?" Sarah asked as she looked up from her notebook. Jim had been temporarily forbidden to buy anymore comics after he spent two hundred dollars on several copies of *Spider-Man* that he claimed he could resell for a huge profit on eBay. He later found out he'd bought the wrong printing and couldn't sell any of them. "Did I say comics? I meant to say something else."

"Like?"

"Shamwow?"

"Nice try, Jim. No comics."

"But Sarah," he whined as Eric laughed in the background.

"NO."

He grimaced as the truck in front of them finished unloading, and he pushed the gas again. "Guess there's no rush to get down there, then. You guys just want to watch the movie early, and we'll go down for the autograph session that Yeti wants to get to?"

"Is that when the chick from *Sasquatch Hunters* will be there?" Eric asked.

"Yep, she's signing at three. So we'll do *Red Dawn* at my place—"

"Oh, not again," she said. "I am so sick of that movie."

"How can anyone get sick of *Red Dawn*?" Jim asked.

"Wolverines!" Eric yelled.

"Never gets old," Jim said, as he smiled and looked at Sarah.

"Have you invited Carol over for Saturday's movie yet?" Eric asked.

Jim cringed.

"What?" Sarah said.

"Whoops, guess not," Eric said. "Let me know how it goes."

Eric hung up as Jim avoided Sarah's look and concentrated on the pineapple air freshener instead.

"Now, before you get mad—"

"Way too late for that," she said, turning towards him and setting her pad on the dashboard.

"We're just trying to set Yeti up with her," he said. "They're both not seeing anyone, and she likes—"

"Hairy morons?" she asked. "Because that's what that guy is. And how do you know she isn't seeing anyone?"

"I, uh, asked her the other day."

Sarah glared at him as he sputtered. "So you did lie to me about why you were out there talking to her?"

"No, I just relayed a different piece of the conversation, that's all. I didn't think it would be a big deal."

"Then why didn't you just tell me?"

"What, I have to give you an in-depth recap of every conversation I have now?"

"If it's with a pretty, young single neighbor who gives you a hard-on, then yes!"

"I told you that was a Kit Kat bar!" He closed his eyes and slowly shook his head. "You don't want her there Saturday, fine. But it wasn't like I was going out there to hit on her."

"It doesn't matter," she said. "I don't like that you're suddenly hiding things from me now, Jimmy. That's twice."

"It won't happen again. I promise." A few minutes passed before he turned right onto Spruce Street into more heavy traffic, this time from road crews. "Hey, the Lady Buttons building is on the right up here," he said and pointed, cruising towards the hospital entrance. "You sure you don't want to meet her? Maybe she and Englebert need a third for Twister."

"Oh, I won't have time—" She paused and grinned at him. "How badly do you want those comic books?"

"Are you kidding? One's this rare *Iron Fist* with—"

"So pretty badly is your answer," she said. "Tell you what. Take that envelope I gave you up to Myrtle, and you can go buy your comics on Saturday."

"That's it?" he asked. "I drop off this stupid button, and you'll let me go? You're up to something."

"Not at all. Just take it up to Myrtle, and you can go."

"Is that so. What exactly is her beef with Cal, anyway?"

"I don't know, what don't you ask her? I'm sure it has nothing to do with some house in Exton."

"I'm sure it has nothing to do with that abandoned funhouse," he said, imitating her voice. "Alright, what about Carol coming over to be setup with the Yeti? You willing to do that too?"

"I'll think about it," she said.

"You'll just think about it?" he asked.

"That's the deal," she said. "Pray that I don't alter it any further."

A huge smile swept across his face as he parked in front of the hospital. He unbuckled his seatbelt and leaned over, hugging and kissing her repeatedly. "A *Star Wars* reference! And you didn't mess it up! You are the greatest!"

"Alright, alright, you silly man," she said, giggling and pushing him off of her. "So you'll do it?"

"Sure, it's a deal. Do you want me to stick around and drive you back to the office?"

"No, I'll probably be awhile," she said. "I'm sure Mr. Donald won't mind if I use the car service to get home."

She kissed him a final time as she hopped out and went inside. He drove back to 1425 Spruce and lucked into a parking spot directly across the street from the building. His parallel parking skills had deteriorated significantly since his days as a student at Temple, evidenced by his four attempts before he finally succeeded in not having his rear tire on the curb. He jogged across the street and looked inside the double doors. A fountain took up most of the lobby. Water cascaded in calming waves over the fake rocks that lined its base as the security guard looked on. The guard was Asian, a bit shorter than Jim, and almost cartoonishly muscular and forbidding, his swelled biceps stretching the limits of his uniform's tight short sleeve shirt.

"So, how's it going?" Jim asked.

"Very well, thank you," the guard answered. "And yourself?"

"Meh, I'm okay. My wife asked me to deliver this to Myrtle in 4B."

The guard looked him and up and down and tapped his chin twice with his right index finger. "Alright, you look harmless enough. Myrtle's up on the second floor." He thumbed towards the elevators. "Just exit the elevator and it's down the hall on the right hand side."

"Second floor?" Jim asked. "Don't you mean fourth floor?"

"No, it's on the second floor."

"But isn't she in office 4B?"

"She is. It's a quirk in the numbering scheme of the building."

"By quirk, do you mean they didn't know how to do it right?"

"Would you like to file a formal complaint?" the guard asked. "Perhaps you'd like to speak to Clarence in our customer service department."

Jim looked at the guard's ID card on his shirt pocket and saw the guard's name was Clarence Yang. The guard slowly nodded when Jim pointed at him.

"No, no complaints."

"Then perhaps it's best if you just take that up now."

He pushed the button for the elevator and followed Clarence's directions to the office. He passed a doctor's office and a tutoring company before he spotted a sign above it that read—

Philadelphia Survey and Research Group—4B

He poked his head in and saw an empty table and a desk with a green lamp and a black telephone. An elderly woman sat at the desk stapling stacks of paper together. He knocked on the open door. "Hi, I'm Jim Knox," he said. "My wife Sarah called earlier and she asked me to drop this off. Are you Myrtle?"

She smiled. "Indeed I am. C'mon in." Jim walked past the table and back to the desk where Myrtle was sitting. "That was so sweet of you to bring this over," Myrtle said, taking the envelope from him and opening it. She pulled out a small pink button that said "Proud Supporter of The New Hollywood" and beamed, holding it up in her hand to admire it. "This is a nice one."

"Yeah, hold onto that," he said, rolling his eyes.

"Well, that was very thoughtful, so thank you," she said. She set the button down on her desk and took a business card out of the drawer. "Here, if Sarah has anymore buttons for me, have her give me a ring. Maybe I can trade her some she doesn't have."

"Oh, you bet." He flipped the card in his hand a few times and stuck it in his wallet.

"Wait, where are you going?" she called after Jim as he turned to leave. "Do you want to stick around and fill out a survey?"

"Yeah, thanks anyway. I really should get going."

"It'll only take about ten minutes. Besides, you get ten dollars just for doing one. What do you say?"

He checked the time on his phone and saw it was just after two. "Ten bucks, huh? I suppose I can do that."

"There's no mobile service in here," she said. "If you need to call someone, you can use the office phone on my desk if you'd like."

"Yeah, no, I'm fine," he said.

"Great, have a seat over at the table." She picked up a clipboard and survey packet from the desk as he took a seat.

"So, today's survey is all about your online shopping habits."

His hand went up. "Question?"

"Yes?"

"You're doing an in-person survey about my online shopping habits?" he asked.

"That's right," she said.

"Doesn't that seem a little strange to you?"

"How so?"

"Well, wouldn't you ask about people's online shopping habits, I don't know, online?"

She tittered and nodded her head. "Of course, I'm just required to get these last few finished up from my old post down at the mall. I got moved here to do outpatient surveys for the hospital once my godson Clarence got a job in this building."

"That security guard in the lobby?" Jim asked, pointing downstairs.

"Yepper-doodle. As soon as I found out he got this job, I got myself assigned to do medical surveys and moved into the only office open, so I could keep my promise. I told Clarence when he was just a munchkin that one day we'd get to work at the same place. And a promise is a promise."

He chuckled. "Is that so?"

"Absolutely, but it does mean business is a little slower than down at the old mall cart, which is fine by me. Gives me more time to get to know my survey victims." She winked, and he laughed again.

"Well then, let's survey it up," Jim said, and she started in on the first question.

After twenty-five minutes of survey questions and small talk, Jim thanked Myrtle and got up to leave. When she checked her watch, she noted it was almost three and decided to call it a day. Jim waited for her as she turned off the light at the desk and collected her purse and jacket.

"Can we just leave through there?" he asked, pointing to the sign on the closed door in the office that read "Warning—Not A Fire Exit."

"Sort of," she said.

"What do you mean?" he asked.

Myrtle walked over to the door. "Here, take a look."

She turned the handle and pushed the door open for him. Inside was a slightly larger room than her office, with a blue and white checked tile floor and a single door on the other side with a crash bar on it. It was dark, and he wouldn't have been able to see anything without the office ceiling's lights.

"You can go out into the hallway through that door over there," she explained, pointing to the other side of the dark room. "But it's not near the stairs or the elevator, so you'd have to walk all the way back around. Can't even come back in that way since the door is missing a doorknob."

"Really? Can't someone fix it?"

"Not only does Cal Nolan and his crummy realty company refuse to fix the doorknob, he has people marching in here every time we have a fire drill."

"A fire drill? Why's that?"

"Because of this nonsense." Myrtle walked back to her desk and pulled out a laminated sheet and handed it to Jim. "This is a copy of the fire evacuation plan each business on the second floor got from Nolan Realty last year."

"Okay," he said, looking it over.

Myrtle walked to the main door and pointed across the hall. "Now, the fire stairs are in that little alcove right over there. But look where the evacuation plan they printed up takes you."

Jim followed Myrtle's finger as it traced the arrow on the sheet through the hallway and into her office.

"It's pointing the wrong way," he said.

"You bet your sweet bippy it is," Myrtle said, shaking her head as she put the evacuation plan away and led them out of the office. "So now I've got a six dollar sign slapped up in my office because Nolan was too cheap to print up new ones."

"Why didn't he put it on the outer door?" he asked as she locked up the office. "You can't even see it now."

"He put it up before I moved in and just left that door open," she said, as they headed downstairs together. "He thought the sign clashed with the aesthetics of the hallway."

Jim chuckled as they entered the lobby and found Clarence still manning his post.

Myrtle approached him and gave him a hug as he asked, "How'd he do, Myrt?"

"Now Clarence, you know I can't tell you that," she said, shaking her finger at him and smiling. "And is that Aqua Velva I smell? I thought you were an Old Spice man."

Clarence put his hands up. "You caught me," he said, grinning. "Wife gave me a bottle for my birthday."

"You're wearing Aqua Velva?" Jim asked him.

"He sure is," she said, giving Clarence a wink. "You can come over and double-check if you don't trust Myrt's old sniffer."

Jim shook his head as Clarence folded his arms and gave Jim a stern look. "No, no I trust you."

"I'd better hurry up. My bus is coming along soon," Myrtle said. "It was great meeting you Jim." He offered her his hand but instead received a warm hug. She hustled outside after blowing them a kiss and got to the bus stop only seconds before it arrived.

"Well if my godmother likes you that much, I guess you're okay," Clarence said, slapping him on the shoulder and causing Jim to wince.

Jim zipped up his light grey jacket to head out. "Hey Clarence, how come you don't just rip that sign down in Myrtle's office for her? That'd be a piece of cake for a guy like you."

"Because someday," Clarence said. "I'm going to watch Cal do it himself."

8

Sarah's feet ached as she slipped her key in the side door lock and opened the door. It was just after seven, and her plan to use the car service instead of having Jim drive her home was ill-advised. The driver never showed, and she had to walk from the hospital to the train station almost a mile away. She missed the 5:30 p.m. express train, and instead had to ride in a middle seat on a local that came by twenty minutes later. The slender hope Jim was making dinner for her was shattered when she saw him hunched over the laptop at the kitchen table pounding his fist and cheering.

"It's on now, Chaka! Eastern Australia is mine! " he shouted.

"Oh please, Jim," she said, tossing her purse on the table. His yell confirmed her fears that he was playing *Risk* online. She slipped off her shoes and sat down next to him, resting her head on his shoulder. "Don't you want to hear how Mr. Donald's doing?"

"Yeah, yeah, in a second, hon. I'm about to take over Iceland."

"Jim, I really was hoping—"

"Woohoo, I won! In your face, pink jerk!"

"Oh would you stop with that for one second and talk to your wife!" she said, slamming the lid to the computer down in one swift motion.

He pulled his hand away just before it snapped shut. "Hey! I was doing something!"

"I'm trying to talk to you, and you're sitting there playing that stupid game. I hate it when you ignore me like that."

"I'm not ignoring you, I was in the middle of something. Another fifteen minutes and I would have won!"

"What's more important, that game or talking to your wife?"

"Hmm. What are you wearing in this scenario?"

"Jim!"

"Okay fine, you're more important buttercup."

"I'm touched."

"I'll touch you all you want, baby," he said in his best Barry White voice as he started tickling her.

"Stop it, I'm not the mood," she said, wresting herself free. "Did you get the text I sent you?"

"Yeah, I got it. Mr. Donald had hemorrhoid surgery, and he's already cracking jokes. I tried calling you a few times, but it went right to voicemail."

"I know, my battery died," she said, retrieving her phone and plugging it into the laptop to recharge. "Would you mind getting a soda or something for me? I'm really thirsty."

"Sure thing." He headed into the kitchen and pulled out two bottles of Yoo-Hoo from the fridge. She made a face as he set one down in front of her. "Here you go," he said.

"I don't want a Yoo-Hoo," she said and pushed it away. "I said I wanted a soda."

"Technically you said you wanted a soda 'or something.' That's 'or something', and it's all we have left."

"You still haven't done the stuff on that list? C'mon Jim, I've asked how you many times to do that now? I knew I should have just gone myself."

"Well I would have, but someone had me delivering a pink button to Myrtle this afternoon. Did you really think that would work?" he asked as he returned her bottle to the fridge.

She curled her lips and shifted her seat. "I don't know what you're talking about," she said, turning towards the laptop.

"I'm talking about your little scheme to make me turn down that job. Well, it's not going to work, Mrs. Knox. I'm still taking it if I win."

"I just wanted you to meet Myrtle. I didn't think you'd actually turn down the job because of her crummy little office."

"Sorry, Sarah, I'm not buying it. You and Lady Buttons probably had this scheme cooked up this morning."

"That's ridiculous," she said and walked over to him. "I told you to mail the envelope at lunch, remember? I didn't know Mr. Donald was going to be admitted to the hospital."

"I don't know, Sarah. I think you'd do anything to win this bet."

"Are you saying you don't believe me?" she asked as she followed him. He stopped and faced her, and she looked directly into her husband's hazel-green eyes. Jim's grimace disappeared after a few moments, and he shook his head.

"Fine, then it's okay if I let Carol come over to meet Yeti on Saturday?" Jim asked. She folded her arms and turned her back to him.

"I haven't decided yet," she said.

He came closer and began massaging her neck and shoulders. She'd always had a weakness for his massages, and her heart rate quickened as he worked the area over again and again.

"You know," he said, kissing her neck. "We don't have to be down here while they're watching the movie."

"We don't?" she asked, pushing her hair away from his face. "But wouldn't that be rude?"

"Oh, I think they'll understand," he said, working his way up her neck to her ears.

"No, we can't Jimmy," she said, looking back at him.

"Why not? I can show them how to work the remote."

"No, I mean now, we can't. You still haven't gotten my sponges like you were supposed to."

"Dammit!" He slumped down into one of the chairs at the kitchen table. "Why didn't you tell me that was on that list, too?"

"I didn't think I had to. You should have at least looked at that list by now if you were serious about store duty."

"I can go right now," he said, hopping out of his chair.

"No, don't, I'm tired. Just make sure you go tomorrow."

"Man, this stinks," he said. "Oh, where's that photo album?"

"Stop it. How about you just make dinner?"

"Yeah, that's the same," he muttered and headed into the kitchen. "Do we still have that leftover ham? I could slice it up and make some sandwiches."

"Sure, that'd be great," she said and sat back down at the computer.

He opened the door and placed condiments and bread on the counter.

"Swiss and spicy mustard for yours, American and jalapeño mustard for mine. Any chips?"

"Just the sandwich, thanks. I can close this game out, right?"

"Yeah, that's fine. What color is the map?"

"Green."

"Man, ChakaKhan730 won AGAIN?"

"You're playing *Risk* online against someone named ChakaKhan730?"

"Chaka's good," he said. "Beaten me and SuckItDark-Warrior199 the last three games."

"Do I dare ask what name you use?"

"Sure, take a look. I was blue."

"You are—" she stopped.

Sarah highlighted his screen name SarahMyLove0406 and smiled. April sixth was their wedding day.

"It was going to be something cool, but I got stuck with that one," he said.

"Mmmhmm." She blew him a kiss when he looked away to finish up the sandwiches. The chimes played as the wall clock hit seven, and she checked her e-mail to kill time as she waited for dinner.

"And . . ." he said, walking into the room with her plate and his. "Your sandwich, my dear. Let me fetch you something to drink." He ran back and got a glass of water from the sink. Placing her glass in front of her, he sat down in the opposite chair and dug in.

"So did Myrtle like the button?" she asked.

"Yeah, she blathered on about it while I took the survey."

"Oh, I didn't think you'd stay and take one. What was it on?"

He put his sandwich down and took some chips from his plate. "My online shopping habits, if you can believe that. It was a pretty dumb survey. Asked a lot of questions about what my last online purchase was and why I chose that store."

"Wasn't your last online purchase this dog humping the USB port you find so hilarious?" she asked, pulling the item for the laptop and tossing it onto the table.

"Yeah, Myrtle thought that was a riot," he said as he picked it up and chuckled.

"Was her office as bad as she told me?"

"I didn't think it was awful, although I can't figure out what that one room was ever used for," he said, scratching the stubble on his chin.

She took another bite and wiped her mouth with her napkin. "She told me she thought it might have been a darkroom, but she wasn't sure."

"Really?" he asked. "Huh, I've never even seen a darkroom before."

"You haven't? I have."

"When was this?"

"I was in photography club in high school for three years," she said.

"Your high school had a photography club? That's weird," he said, finishing up the last of his chips.

"Weird? I'm pretty sure lots of high schools had a photography club."

"I don't think mine did. I don't think my high school had any clubs."

"No way. Some of my favorite memories were from my high school clubs." She leaned her head in her hand and smiled. "I should really look some of my old classmates up. Maybe my class has a reunion page or something."

"Yeah, cause nothing says fun like seeing how everyone from high school fell apart after fifteen years," he said, finishing his sandwich and searching for his napkin. "Hey, check out Joe Schmoe, he really got bald, didn't he?"

Sarah lifted up his plate and handed his napkin to him. "Are you saying I fell apart?"

"No way, Dorian Gray. You're the only person I know who looks exactly the same. If people saw your yearbook photo they'd think you struck a deal with the devil."

"I still haven't seen your yearbook, ever. Do you even have it anymore?"

"I think so," he said, leaning back in his chair. "It's probably packed down in a box in the basement somewhere."

"Go see if you do. I want to see this high school with no clubs you went to."

"I'm not going down there by myself. It's spooky and spidery down there."

"You are such a fraidy-cat," she said. "Fine, I'll go down with you."

"Well since you're going down now, maybe it's best if I just wait here. I mean—"

She grabbed his ear and pulled him up from the chair as it came back to the ground. He winced as she pulled him away and followed her down to the basement. She flicked on the light and pulled a hair band from her pocket, pulling her brown hair back into a ponytail as they crept down the creaky steps.

"I don't know why you don't believe me. And just so you know, eighth grade wasn't considered high school at my school. It started in ninth grade," he said as he poked through the maze of boxes that lined the floor.

"Eighth grade wasn't high school for me either. That was the last year I was in baseball card club."

"You traded baseball cards?" he asked. "Bet that was something to watch."

"What's that supposed to mean?"

"I know how you are. Let me guess—every time you made a trade, you'd pull out some stupid magazine to tell you what each card was worth, because god forbid you traded a ten cent card for an eight cent card."

"What's wrong with that?" she asked.

"Well nothing if you don't mind missing out on stuff just because it isn't 'fair' on paper. I remember a trade I made where I had to give the kid some George Brett card worth ten bucks for a Reggie Jackson card worth ten cents."

"Then why'd you do the deal?"

"It was for Reggie Jackson," he said and pulled down another box from the shelf. "You can't put a price on Reggie."

"Yes, you can," she said, folding her arms. "And Reggie Jackson was never a Phillie. Why'd you like him so much?"

"Because he was supposed to be drafted by the Mets, and they blew it. Anyone who makes the Mets look stupid is my hero."

"It's still a bad trade. I never would have made a deal like that."

"No kidding. That's why Mr. Whiskers is still sitting in the pet shop window." A few weeks ago, the pet store at the mall by their house got a new orange and white kitten in the window. She'd fallen in love with him the first time they walked by.

"Aww, poor Mr. Whiskers. He has that cute little meow he makes when he sees me."

"He's just yawning."

"No he isn't! He does that thing with his paws too." She pawed at the air like Mr. Whiskers while Jim shook his head.

"See, you obviously really want that stupid cat. Just get him already," Jim said.

"Not if it means signing up for your ridiculous 'Felines for Frederick's' program." For years, he'd begged her to buy lingerie from Frederick's of Hollywood, but she'd turned him down every time, claiming it was too trashy.

"Fine, but if you ever want Reggie Jackson, I gotta have that George Brett," he said, rifling through the box.

"Oh, I think I found it," she said as she pulled out the light green yearbook from the box. "That's clever. What is that on the cover, a Muppet?"

"Kind of. Jim Henson died maybe a year or two before I graduated, so they decided to do a whole Muppet theme."

"Which one is on the cover? I don't recognize him."

"He's not really a Muppet. The cost to use actual Muppets was really expensive, so that's a fake one. We had to make up names for them in a contest sponsored by Yearbook . . . dammit!"

She smirked but didn't respond, flipping open the cover and casually leafing through the pages.

"Alright, fine, we had clubs," he said, trying to take it from her as she headed upstairs. They reached the landing and walked across the living room as she found his yearbook picture. Jim looked much like he did when they first met, minus the muttonchops. She flipped to the index and leaned against the couch.

"Except for this one picture, you're barely in here. Didn't you play any sports?"

"Nope, weak ankles."

"Band? Chorus?"

"Double no. God what kind of loser did band or chorus?"

"I did, Jim. I was pretty good too."

"Sure you were."

"What? I was."

"I've heard you sing. It's like listening to a cat being gutted by a screeching canary. I've never fully recovered from you rendition of 'Fields of Gold.' Sting must be rolling over in his grave."

"Sting's not dead."

"He would be if he heard you kill that song."

"At least I tried!" she said defiantly as she leafed through the pages. "Oh, here's drama guild. I always wanted to try acting."

"Ohhh—the *guild*. Aren't we so important, drinking our flagons of mead and toasting our queen of overacting and hamminess."

"You might have enjoyed it if you weren't so cynical."

"Give me a break. Look at the losers in here. What the hell is the girl doing in that picture?"

"She's having fun, Jim. You know, fun?"

"It's doesn't look like fun. Looks like she's about to eat that other woman's brains. What kind of sick plays did my school put on anyway?"

"It says here that's from the production of *The Crucible*. I love that play."

"Oh man, now I remember that chick," he moaned. "She was in my homeroom. That's all she jabbered on about for months."

"What'd that poor girl ever do to you? I'd have been excited if I was starring in the school play too. Just because she talked about it to her friends you're all mad at her?"

"It wasn't just that. I had to hear about her being secretary of the guild and then acting in some stupid musical called *Chess*. Whoever heard of *Chess*? And what does the secretary do in the drama guild, anyway? Other than pretend to be important by calling herself secretary, I mean."

Sarah slammed the book closed and tucked it under her arm. She walked over to the bookcase next to their television and pulled out a DVD that she slapped on his chest.

"What's this?"

"That's the official DVD from Royal Albert Hall in London of the original Broadway cast's production of *Chess*. It's one of my all-time favorite musicals, which I would have thought my husband would have known. And since I was secretary in the clubs I was in, I can tell you not only is it the hardest job, it's one of the most important. So guess what, my inconsiderate jerk of a husband? You're going to sit your ass down on that couch and watch the entire two-and-half-hours of *Chess*, the musical!"

"Are you serious? Oh c'mon I—"

"Jim, one more word out of you, and you're going to be sleeping on that couch instead of just watching *Chess* on it!"

Jim slinked to his seat like a child. He fell into the middle cushion and toppled on his side. She put the DVD in and walked over to the kitchen table to clean up.

"You're not even watching?" he asked.

"No, I have a lot of work to do tonight with my little Cal Nolan case because I'm reading books at the library tomorrow morning," she said, throwing out their trash and putting the dishes in the dishwasher. "Remember?"

"Oh yeah," he said and rubbed his mouth. "Have fun with that."

She walked back from the kitchen and stood in front of the TV, staring at him. "Why don't you come along and help your wife out since Mr. Donald can't make it?"

"Nah, big day tomorrow," he said, straining to see around her. "First, I'm going to watch *Chess 2: Electric Boogaloo* and then—"

"But you're great with kids," she pointed out. "I bet you'd have fun with it. The library is only two miles from the river-front."

"Oh, Ben's Hot Dog stand?" he asked, sitting up and looking at her. On their second date they discovered Ben's and the best hot dogs in Philly. They'd shared their first kiss on a nearby bench and made it a point to go back at least once a year ever since.

"If that's what you want."

"I'm in," he said, "Now, shh, get out of the way. This guy's about to sing 'King Me'."

"You don't king someone in—never mind," she said, rolling her eyes as Jim bobbed his head to the music.

9

Jim looked out at the creeping line of red brake lights on the expressway in front of them and leaned on his horn. A light rain tapped on the roof of their Altima as they inched along the expressway. Traffic had been heavy ever since they'd left the house around 9:00 a.m. and was getting worse the closer they got to Center City. "C'mon," he said.

Sarah looked up from the manila folder in her lap and went straight back to work. Twirling a pink highlighter with her fingers, she pored through various news articles she'd printed out about Cal Nolan. "Just stay in this lane," she said as she marked the text. "What's your rush?"

"I'm bored. We've been sitting in traffic since we left, and you won't talk to me or let me listen to the radio."

"I didn't say you couldn't listen to the radio, just not to WIP." The Philadelphia sportstalk radio station always induced Jim to yell back at the various callers.

"But I can listen to Stern?"

"Yes, you can to listen to Stern."

He glanced at the clock on the dashboard and banged his hand on the steering wheel. "Dammit, it's past 9:30. I missed the spitting contest."

"A spitting contest on the radio?"

"Yep, he was having Baba Booey and some chicks from *Penthouse* see who could spit the furthest. I betcha anything Baba Booey won."

She nodded and flipped to the next page in her stack. "Probably right."

He left the radio off, instead drumming his hands on the steering wheel and bobbing his head as he hummed.

She recognized the tune and smirked. "That's from *Chess*," she said.

"Yeah, sorry, just excited about tonight, that's all."

"Oh are you?" she asked.

"Sure, I mean either you win the bet, and I get to have sex, or you lose the bet, and I get to have sex. Either way I'm having sex."

"Sex wasn't part of our bet."

"No, but it should have been. Who cares? We're still having it, aren't we?"

"Well, yeah," she said. "But make sure you pick up alcohol later. I'm going to want to be drunk either way."

"Ah, just like our first time," he said, puckering up as he leaned over to kiss her. She smiled and pushed his face away from her. "So when I win, which are you hoping for, Cal or Texas?" he asked.

"I'm hoping Cal moves to Texas," she said. She snapped the cap back on the highlighter and set the folder on the floor.

"What are you doing?"

"I'm obviously not going to finish reading this right now," she said. "Turn on the news or something." She picked up her purse and pulled down her visor mirror.

"Are you sure?" he asked. She checked her makeup and closed it back up without making any adjustments.

"Yes, it was just some fluff interview Cal Nolan did with *Philadelphia Magazine*. They asked a bunch of silly questions like if you could have dinner with any three dead people, who would they be? Stuff like that."

He snapped his fingers. "Got it!"

"Got what?"

"Who my three people would be. Gerald Ford, Wilt Chamberlain, and you."

"Me? I'm not dead!"

"You think I'm going to a dinner like that and not bring you along? Screw that. Who's Cal bringing?"

Jim weaved through the now faster moving traffic. "His parents. So you'd pass up the opportunity to go to a dinner like that if I couldn't come along?" she asked.

"Of course," he said. "Why, don't you want to go?"

She took his free hand with hers and smiled. "No, I'd love to come. I think it's sweet you're having President Ford along, so I can meet Betty."

"I didn't know you liked Betty," he said. "But Gerald's my boy."

"Are you kidding me?" she asked, pulling her hand away. "I've always loved Betty Ford. I dressed up like her on Halloween once."

"When was this?"

"When I was in first grade," she said. "My mom even sewed me a little wig to wear."

"Huh," he said, taking her hand again. "I had no idea."

"Well, I had no idea Gerald was your boy, either."

"That guy was awesome," he said as he sat up in his seat. "He was a star football player, got to marry a hot dancer, and then became president. How cool is that?"

"You're too much," she said. "Most people would pick Abraham Lincoln or George Washington or someone like that."

"What am I going to talk to those two about?" he asked. "Oh, look at me, I'm George Washington. I quelled the Whiskey Rebellion. Lame. I'd rather swap stories with Gerald about telling New York to drop dead."

"Wouldn't you rather swap stories about him pardoning Nixon?"

"Not really, although I do want to watch a story they did on the *TODAY* show about presidential pardons that had him in it. Do we still have that one recorded?"

"I'm sure we do," she said. "Well do you mind if I ask him about it then?"

"What do you want do that for? I'd rather just let him eat," he said.

"But don't you want to know why—"

"Know why he showed compassion when everyone wanted a spectacle?" Jim asked, watching the road but turning towards her to give his response. "Why he put the country's best interests above his own? Why he knew that compassion is sometimes a better answer than vengeance?" He ticked off each point in rapid succession, punctuating them with his hand cutting through the air.

"Except Nixon never even said he was sorry. Doesn't that bother you?"

"Who are you, David Frost? Of course it would have been nice if Tricky Dick had just come out and said it, but sometimes you have to be the better man. And if you want to spend the whole meal badgering him about it—"

"Alright, alright, calm down," she said, putting her hand on his leg. "My god, what got into you?"

He took a deep breath and rolled his head around a few times. "How would you like it if your idol lost to a peanut farmer because he made the right decision? It's just a sore subject, that's all."

"Weren't you two-years-old when that election happened?"

"And I've carried that pain with me ever since. Just ask Wilt something instead, okay?"

"You know what?" she asked. "Let's just double with the Fords. I'm sure Wilt's already got a date that night anyway."

He chuckled as she clicked on the radio to listen to the local news channel. The rain had picked up and bounced noisily off the hood of the car. Jim clicked to another channel playing Bruce Springsteen.

"Why'd you change it?" she asked. "I wanted to hear traffic and weather on the two's."

"It's raining, and I'm getting off at this exit. Report filed."

He whistled the news radio theme song as they got off the expressway, winding through the back streets of Fishtown in Philadelphia. The rundown homes and shops that lined the street were quiet, and they passed a couple groups from local companies building a playground in the steady rain. Another volunteer group was in the library parking lot when they arrived, giving free flu shots under a blue tent. The line of people waiting snaked all the way back to the road.

They ran inside and Sarah folded up her blue and white Villanova umbrella. Jim shook himself off as she checked her navy blue pantsuit for any stray raindrops and headed into the bathroom. Several people sipped coffee and read magazines at the few tables that lined the wall.

A young male librarian approached Jim as he entered the main level and read the sign welcoming the various groups. "Are you a reading volunteer?" the librarian asked.

"Um, I guess? I'm with my wife from Donald and Kim," he said. "She's in the bathroom right now."

"Okay great. If you want to head downstairs when she returns, there's a volunteer already reading to the kids, and you'll be up when he's finished."

"Alright," said Jim. The librarian nodded and walked over to take care of a patron waiting at the information desk. Sarah returned from the bathroom, and they walked downstairs.

They found a large group of toddlers and their parents all listening intently to a reading of *The Cat in the Hat* by a chubby, middle-aged male volunteer. The man seemed to enjoy his role, enunciating every passage and making funny faces as the children tittered and giggled each time. They cheered as he came to the end, and he took an exaggerated bow.

"Thank you, Mr. Matt!" an older Asian woman said and shook his hand. "Wow, that's going to be a tough act to follow." She pulled out an index card and ran her finger down the middle. "Are Sarah Knox and Frank Donald here yet?"

Sarah raised her hand. "I'm Sarah Knox," she said. "Mr. Donald's not feeling well and couldn't make it, but my husband Jim will be reading in his place."

"Well, that's wonderful. Who'd like to go first, you or your husband?"

"I'll go," he said, kissing Sarah on the cheek and walking over to the circle of children.

"Alright kids, can we give Mr. Jim a big round of applause?"

The kids cheered as Jim walked to the reader's seat and blew kisses to the crowd. Sarah laughed and shook her head.

"Okay kids, Mr. Jim is going to be reading one of my favorite books, *The Little Baby Snoogle-Fleejer*!" said the librarian.

Jim smiled as he took the book from her, but his grin disappeared as he read the front cover and saw who the author was.

"I'm not reading that," he said and handed it back to the woman. The librarian gave him a funny look as Sarah walked over to join them. The three of them huddled away from the circle so the kids couldn't hear them.

"There's no reason to be nervous," she whispered to him. "You'll be fine."

He pointed at the front cover. "I'm not reading any book written by Jimmy Carter. Give me something else."

"Is he serious?" the librarian asked.

"Give me that," Sarah said and took the book from the librarian. "I'll read it. He can read the one I was supposed to." Jim excused himself and walked to the back of the room as the children looked on. He went to the computer workstation in the corner as Sarah introduced herself and started reading. After Googling his own name and checking his e-mail for a few minutes, the chubby man who'd read previously came up to him and leaned against the desk.

"Don't sweat it," he told Jim, "It's always hard your first time in front of a live audience. But you'll get the hang of it."

"It's not that, it's—never mind."

"Your wife sounds like she's doing alright. Maybe she could give you some pointers."

"I'm fine, really." Jim shifted his chair away from the other man.

"Hey, want to see something cool?" Matt snatched the keyboard from Jim and did a search on Amazon.com. "Check it out—it's the book I just self-published."

"*Ghimes?*" Jim asked, as he looked at the screen.

"Yeah, cool title, huh?"

"Not really," Jim said as he took the keyboard back. The audience began applauding as Sarah finished reading.

"Ah, but you haven't heard the premise."

"Look, no offense, but if it's self-published, I'm guessing it's not all that compelling."

"See, that's where you're wrong. It's a mystery novel that starts out with a boy who learns to play piano, and then goes on a killing spree because his piano teacher was really an alien who anally probed him after every lesson."

"That's awful!" Sarah said as she approached from behind them. She pointed to Jim that it was his turn as the librarian led the kids in a quick stretching exercise.

"You just wait, *Ghimes* is going to be huge. If publishers weren't too busy publishing crap like that *Big Red Machine* book I read today, maybe they'd have time for books like *Ghimes*." Matt grabbed his bookbag from the railing as he stomped out.

He cocked his head and made eye contact with Sarah, who was grinning as she took his place in front of the computer.

"Sarah, you can't honestly—"

"You just worry about your book," she said, pointing towards the circle of children.

The librarian directed the kids to sit back down as Jim walked up to her, and she handed him a copy of *Green Eggs and Ham*. He grinned and hugged her as the kids laughed. Instead of sitting back down in the chair, he acted out each of the parts as the kids roared at his voices and mannerisms. As he finished up to rapturous applause and bowed, he strutted over to Sarah and put his hand in between her face and the computer screen she was reading.

"I killed!" he said, offering her the high five. He shook it when she failed to look up from the screen. "Sarah? Hello? High Five?"

"C'mon, I'm trying to do something," she said, pushing his hand out of her face.

"Hey, what's your problem?" he asked. "I just got a standing O."

"Damn it, I can't find it," she said, standing and heading over to the librarian who waited as some of the kids took a bathroom break before the next speaker.

"Sarah, what are you doing?" he asked as he followed her over.

"Excuse me," Sarah asked her. "Can I ask you about a book that gentleman Matt read called *Big Red Machine?*"

"Oh that," the librarian said. "That was part of a special donation we just got in. I'm sure it would have made Mr. Scanlon happy that we—"

"Scanlon?" Sarah asked.

God, here we go, he thought.

"That's right. Gary Scanlon, from Scanlon's Publishing. Mr. Scanlon had written several books he never published, and when he died, the company gave us all the proof copies he'd made."

"Did he have any family? A daughter?"

"No, no family that I know of. There's a little bio in each of his books, though." The librarian got up and shuffled over to a stack of books on the shelf behind them and took one. "Here. *Big Red Machine and the Big Race* by Gary Scanlon. Enjoy."

"Thank you," Sarah said, walking back towards the computer.

"What the hell is that?" he asked, pointing at the poorly drawn cover that showed a misshaped cartoon fire engine triumphantly crossing the finish line, running on a pair of wheels.

"Didn't you hear?" she said. "She said a Gary Scanlon wrote this."

"Yeah, I heard. It's just a coincidence."

"You think it's just a coincidence that someone named Scanlon did a book called *Big Red Machine and the Big Race?* It could be a lead."

"Well, since the librarian just said he didn't have any kids, I'm pretty sure it's not a lead. C'mon, let's go to Ben's," he said, trying to take her hand and head upstairs.

"She only thought he didn't have any kids," she said and pulled her hand from his grasp. "I'm not convinced."

"Oh you're not, are you?" he asked.

"No. I don't have to be at the office until one, so I'm not leaving just yet."

His teeth ground together as she sat down. "And what about our lunch at Ben's?"

She glanced at her watch and shook her head. "It's already past eleven, so it's probably going to be too tight. Maybe if we're lucky, we'll have time to get something and go, but—"

"You're a piece of work," he said. "We'll have fun, because I'm leaving and going to Ben's." He headed upstairs and heard her calling for him as he pushed past several other patrons on the staircase.

"Wait," she said, finally getting close enough to grab his arm as they reached the lobby. "I can't believe you're really going to leave me here."

"Watch me." He shoved his hands in his pockets and headed out to the parking lot and past the line of people waiting in the rain for flu shots. She struggled to keep up in her heels and barely had time to open her umbrella.

"Would you slow down? Why are you so mad all of the sudden?" she asked.

"Are you fucking kidding me? I'm sick of putting up with this shit!" He glanced over at the line of people trying not to watch as he got back to the car.

Sarah tried to get the umbrella over him, and he pushed it away from his head. "Stop it, you're making a scene," she said.

"I'm making a scene? I'm not the one grasping at straws in there so I can keep my husband down the rest of his life."

"Hey! That is not true! All I've ever wanted is what's best for you."

"Bullshit," he said, pointing at her. "You only want what's best for Sarah. God, you are so fucking selfish."

"How could you ever accuse me of that? All I'm trying to do is follow-up on—"

He pounded the back of the Altima with his fist. "It's not a fucking lead. You're so desperate to ruin this for me—"

"You offered this deal to me!" She brushed his head with the umbrella. He again pushed it away from her. "And you don't see me screaming about you spending half your time these days sneaking around and fantasizing about younger women."

"I haven't been doing that and you know it!"

"Oh do I? First it was Carol, and then you buy me those shoes because you had another Kit Kat moment when you saw Jane wearing them."

"You know what? Go to hell, Sarah. All you want is someone you can keep a short leash on who is never more successful than you. God forbid I get to be a real man with a real job again."

"A real man wouldn't be leering at younger women and bitching because his wife is successful at something!"

"Please. Some success story. I bet you drive everyone nuts down there with your folders and spreadsheets and color-coded charts. You know what? Why don't you quit that job if you have such a problem with Cal Nolan?"

"Quit?"

"Well, Cal's one of your company's biggest clients, right? You shouldn't want to work for a firm that takes money from a bad man like Cal Nolan."

"That's not the same thing! He offered you a bribe to cover—"

"See? Exactly. Sarah gets to work at a company that does business with Cal but not her husband. But it doesn't matter, because I'm calling my brother and taking that job in Texas. At least I'll be the hell away from you."

"You're not going anywhere," she said, poking him in his chest. "We have a bet."

"Give it a rest, Nancy Drew," he said, swatting her hand off of him. "You were never going to win our bet and—"

She poked him in the chest again as she spoke. "Oh you think so, huh?"

"I know so!"

"Well not only am I going to win this bet, I'm gonna rub your smartass nose in it every time you even think about unwrapping your Kit Kat bar with me. Because the only action you'll be getting for the next ten years is when you leer at Carol's cleavage every Halloween."

He leaned right into her face. "No problem there. At least Carol still gets me hard."

She slapped him.

He rubbed his face, saw her eyes well and shook his head as he stepped out from under the umbrella. "Fine, take the fucking car and investigate all you want." He dropped the keys at her feet in a small pool of dirty water.

Her eyes narrowed, and she bent down to pick them up. He turned to leave the parking lot and said, "But you won't win."

10

Sarah sat back down at the computer terminal downstairs when she got inside, furious and more determined to win than ever. She pounded on the keys, frustrated she couldn't find evidence to incriminate Cal Nolan. The assistant at Mr. Flynn's office knew he owned the house and assured her there were no issues with the Exton home, and after hours of poring through documents last night, she'd found nothing suspicious. She did a quick check of her e-mail and voicemail messages, then flipped through the *Big Red Machine and the Big Race*, cringing at the quality of the writing. The stanza on the third page read—

Big Red Machine
Is Falling Behind
The Race Is Still Going
And He's Still Behind

No wonder he never published himself, she thought and set the book down on the table. She turned back to the computer and Googled Gary Scanlon, pulling out the pen she only used for special occasions. She realized it was one Jim had given her when she'd gotten her current job, and she threw it in the trash can before pulling out another, which Jim had also bought as a backup in case she ever lost the first. *Whatever*, she said to herself and jotted down some notes in her pad.

Her heart sunk a bit when she read Gary Scanlon's obituary and learned he'd never been married. Originally born and raised in Cincinnati, he moved to Philadelphia after college and started his own company called Scanlon Publishing, which specialized in children's books. It was a small operation of about twenty-five people or so, and he personally approved every book they published. He died early last year of prostate cancer at age sixty-six and had a small funeral with military honors for his service in Vietnam. He'd resisted being bought out by a larger firm, but there was talk that a merger with a larger publishing house was now inevitable.

The company website she found hadn't been updated in months. It showed basic information about the company, but several of the pictures didn't load, and the address and phone number didn't match the ones listed in her first search. A note on the website asked visitors to send all correspondence to their new address. It was on the fourth floor of an office building along the Delaware River, not far from the library. Their old address was 1425 Spruce Street in Office 3A, which they'd apparently moved out of eighteen months ago.

1425 Spruce Street? No way that's a coincidence, she thought. She called the current phone number, but it went directly to a generic voicemail message. Her phone showed the time as 11:45 a.m. when she slung her leather purse over her shoulder and walked out to the Altima. The engine roared to life as Sarah pushed the ignition and dialed Frank Donald's room at the hospital. He'd asked her to check-in when she'd finished at the library.

"Hello?" he answered, sounding a little tired.

"Good morning, Mr. Donald," she said, trying to sound upbeat as she adjusted her seatbelt and pulled into traffic.

"Oh, I'm glad it's you, Mrs. Knox. How did it go at the library?"

"It went very well, thank you. We both read a book and the kids really seemed to enjoy it."

"You both did?"

"Yes, my husband came along in your place. I hope that was alright."

"Well, that's wonderful. So were you both surprised?"

She turned the volume up on the phone. "Surprised?"

"Yes. By the book I had them pick out for you to read."

"Did you pick out *The Little Baby Snoogle-Fleejer* or *Green Eggs and Ham*?"

There was silence on the other end.

"Mr. Donald?"

"That is just typical. I specifically called and said they were to have you read *Fox in Socks*."

"I'm so sorry, they didn't say anything to me. We just read what they handed to us."

"And I was so hoping to surprise you. I thought you'd find that funny since there's a Mr. Knox in the book."

She laughed as she turned on the one-way street leading to the riverfront. "I would have Mr. Donald. That's very clever of you."

"Well, as long as the children had fun. So what are you up to the rest of your day off?"

"Day off?"

"That was the other surprise. You are to take the rest of the day off. If I'm stuck in this silly electric bed, you should have some time to relax."

"But Mr. Donald, I can't just—"

"That is an order, Mrs. Knox. Everyone should be doing volunteer work today anyway, so whatever comes up can wait till tomorrow morning. You'll be at the hospital at nine for my conference call with Mr. Kim tomorrow, correct?"

"Yes, I'll be there, Mr. Donald. You sure you don't want me—"

"No, and goodbye, Mrs. Knox. Please turn your Blueberry off too."

"Thank you, Mr. Donald." She half-smiled as he hung up, glad to have plenty of time to go to Scanlon's and ask around. Her smile vanished as she passed Ben's Hot Dog Stand on the right-hand side of the road. The rain had turned to a fine mist, and she maneuvered into the underground parking garage of Scanlon Publishing's office building. She tried calling the publisher a second time, and again there was just the voicemail message. The garage was fairly empty, and she was able to park by the staircase to the main lobby. She brushed her hair and re-applied her lip gloss and rouge before heading upstairs.

The door to Scanlon Publishing's group of offices on the fourth floor was slightly ajar when she arrived. She entered the waiting area that looked a little like a doctor's office, complete with a reception desk behind a small glass window. Various books the company had apparently published were displayed in the lobby, but she didn't recognize any of them.

"Hello?" she asked, peering through the open glass window. A red-haired man with headphones on worked at a cubicle in the back. She pounded on the glass to get his attention, startling him as he turned in his chair. Giving a small wave, he set his headphones on the desk and hurried over to greet her. He was close to six-and-a-half-feet tall, and had a thick build. He sported a goatee and bags under his eyes. The window slid open, and he leaned against the counter, peering out at her.

"Sorry about that," he said. "I thought all the appointments for today had been cancelled."

"Oh, I don't have an appointment," Sarah said. "If the office is closed, I can—"

"No, no worries, I'm just catching up on some stuff while everyone's out, and it's quiet for once. I'm Jeff Clay. I'm a senior editor here."

"Hi, I'm Sarah Knox," she said as they shook hands.

"So, what can do I for you, Sarah?"

"I, um, I know this is a longshot, but I'm looking for someone called Jane Scanlon. Is there anyone who was related to Gary with that name?"

He coughed and shook his head. "No, Gary didn't have any family. He was a loner."

"And I'm guessing no one worked here with that name either?"

"Nope," he said, scratching the back of his neck. "Never had another Scanlon, and I've been here going on twenty years. Anything else?"

She froze, but she was sure she'd spotted the man's tell. *I'll show Jimmy.* She grinned and prepared her bluff. "There is another name she uses. You see, Jane Scanlon isn't her real name. But I can't tell you it since she's a very private person."

The man patted his cheek and looked her over. "Is that right?"

"Maybe if I described her for you. She's a very pretty girl, about five foot ten, a hundred and twenty pounds. Blonde hair, brown eyes, little scar on her hand. Has anyone worked here who looked like that?"

"Goddammit!" He slammed his fist down on the desk, startling her. "That asshole won't quit. I thought we were done with this bullshit."

Her heart beat a mile a minute as she watched his face get redder. "Look, I don't want any trouble, I'm just—"

"I don't want to fucking hear it," Jeff said. "You disgust me even more than he does."

She panicked and ran towards the door, but he rushed out from behind the reception area and physically blocked her from exiting. She retreated back into the room, stumbling as he towered over her.

"You're not just walking out of here. I'm not letting Bob find her again."

"Please, I've made a mistake," she said, cowering. "I'm not here to—"

He leaned over, and she could feel his hot breath on her face. "You're not here to what?"

"I'm not here to hurt Jane. Please, I, I just met her the other day out in Exton."

"Sure you did. Let me ask you, how can you live with yourself? A woman taking money to help a wife beater track down someone. It's inhuman."

"I swear, I have no idea what you're talking about. I only saw her on Sunday for a minute after my husband helped Cal Nolan with some problem with the cable."

He straightened up as he heard this and shook his head. "I don't believe you."

"No, it's true, you can ask him yourself."

"Oh I will," he said and pointed to a wooden chair along the wall. "Go sit your ass down."

She brushed her hair out of her face, frightened and confused. Jeff picked up the phone on the desk and pulled a business card out of his wallet. He punched in the number as Sarah took the seat he'd directed her to.

"God help you if you're lying to me," he growled, pressing the phone against his ear. "Hi Bonnie, it's Jeff Clay. Well, I'm not sure, can you just have Cal call me as soon as he can? Have him call the private office number. Okay, thanks." He set the phone back down and pulled a chair up in front of her. "Hand me your purse."

He grabbed it from her trembling hand and pulled out her large black wallet. There were several pictures of her and Jim in addition to some credit cards, business cards and her driver's license. Jeff took the license out of the sleeve along with one of her business cards and tossed the wallet back in her bag.

"Sarah Knox, brown hair, lives out in Springfield. Your business card says you work at Donald and Kim?"

"Yes, I'm Mr. Donald's assistant."

"Okay, Sarah Knox, let's say you're not here trying to track Karen down for her ex-husband. Why are you digging around about her then?"

She took a deep breath and told the truth. "I was just trying to prove to my husband that Cal was hiding something."

"Yeah, he's helping hide a girl who had the hell beat of out her. What were you hoping he was hiding? An affair?"

She dropped her head and closed her eyes. It was more difficult to explain to someone other than Jim. "No, well, not really, it's more complicated than that."

"You do realize that was his wife I was speaking to just now. She knows all about Karen or Jane or whatever she's been forced to call herself these days. Boy you're either a really shitty detective or—" She was saved from any further tongue-lashing when the phone rang.

Jeff answered the phone, "Scanlon—oh hey Cal. I've got a Sarah Knox here, supposedly works over at Donald and Kim as Frank Donald's assistant. She showed up today snooping around about Karen, and I pegged her as one of Bob's detectives. Claims not only that she isn't, but that she met you and Karen on Sunday along with her husband out in Exton."

Jeff looked at her and nodded. "Yeah, that's her - huh - Well, she claims she was trying to prove to her husband you were hiding something - Okay, hold on." He beckoned Sarah to come to the phone. "He wants to talk to you." She rose from her chair and walked slowly to the desk, wiping her hands along her pants and taking the receiver from Jeff.

"Hello?"

"So you couldn't leave well enough alone, could you, Hollywood?"

"I'm sorry, I didn't know . . ."

"No, of course you didn't. You're too busy running around with your head up your ass. I sacrificed a lot to help Karen, and you come along and fuck everything up by poking around. Now I'm going to have to move her again, I suppose."

"I thought you were trying to bribe my husband, that's all. I shouldn't have been so—"

"Save it. I run into morons like you all the time that don't know the real Cal Nolan. I thought you were a pill on Sunday but man, I had no idea your husband was putting up with this. He should leave a nightmare like you while he's got the chance."

Her lips quivered as he continued his tirade. The tears she had successfully held back formed in her eyes. She'd never been dressed down so harshly in her entire life.

"And to top it off, you work for that idiot Frank Donald. Figures that old fool would hire a moron like you to be his wet-nurse. Surprised he even has his shoes on the right feet with you running the show." Jeff handed her a tissue box. She took a tissue and dabbed at her eyes.

"So run along now, and I'll call Jim and let him know why he lost out on that big signing bonus I just worked out for him."

"No, please don't do that," she pleaded.

"I don't have much of a choice now, do I? I can't have you running around playing *Nancy Drew* at the TBQ Christmas party."

"I won't. I promise."

"Tell you what, I'm a generous guy. Say pretty please, Calvin."

She wiped away the tears on her cheeks and looked away from Jeff.

"Pretty please, Calvin," she whispered.

"I can't hear you," he taunted.

"Pretty please, Calvin."

"That's better. I'll think about it, Hollywood. Now give Jeff the phone. If you can handle that."

She handed the phone back to Jeff and sniffled and wiped her eyes. He wiped the receiver off on his shirt as she blew her nose and collected her things.

"Yeah Cal. Mmmhmm. Mmmhmm. Okay, I will. Thanks." Jeff hung up the phone and leaned against the desk, crossing his arms and watching her wipe her tears. "Cal confirmed your story. He said I should show you something before you go." Jeff disappeared into the back office, returning a few moments later with a sheet of paper he handed to her.

"That's a copy of the restraining order against Karen's ex-husband Bob," he said. Sarah briefly read the paper he gave her and handed it back to him. It stated Karen Scanlon had a restraining order against her husband Robert Rauck for a host of reasons including domestic violence and stalking.

"I'm sorry I kind of flipped out there, but he's tried every trick in the book. Three or four other detectives have already been around in the last few months, and we're not going to let him hurt Karen anymore. She's been in hiding for a year now using various aliases, but he keeps coming after her."

"I should go," Sarah said. She shoved the crumpled tissues in her purse. He opened the door for her and stood aside.

"Cal's quite a guy. Thank god he helped her," he said.

Each step back to the car felt like she was walking through mud. She opened the car door and collapsed in her seat, exhausted. She tried calling Jim, but it went straight to his voicemail.

"Hi, this is Jim Knox, and you've reached my cell. My wife Sarah has the key. Ha ha!"

The phone beeped for her to leave a message.

"You win, Jimmy. You win."

11

Jim stepped out of the taxi onto his driveway as the driver waved and sped off. It had stopped raining and the sun peeked out, but the weather did little to change his disposition. While he was still furious, storming off hadn't helped as much as he'd hoped. He'd gotten soaked, ruined his phone by dropping it in a puddle, and forgotten to take his house keys off his key ring before tossing them at Sarah's feet.

He took a seat on the bumper of his van. He banged his fist against the rear door several times, still angry about their fight. *Why doesn't she want me to be happy?* He removed the spare van key from underneath the rear wheel well and unlocked the driver's door to hit the garage door opener.

"Mr. Jim! Mr. Jim!" Carol's five-year-old daughter Marianne yelled as she ran up the sidewalk towards him. He always found it amusing how excited she got to see him and his "neat truck."

"Hi Marianne," said Jim. Carol came jogging out of her townhouse three doors down in a LaSalle University sweatshirt and black leggings. Her cropped brown hair, which was much shorter than it used to be, was still very flattering, and her Native American heritage gave her skin an almost chestnut color.

"I'm so sorry, Jim. She's been looking out the window every couple minutes to see if you'd come home," she said. "I told her I didn't know when you'd be here." Marianne tugged furiously at his sleeve.

"That's alright," he said. "So what can I do for you, young lady?"

"Can you fix the TV?" Marianne asked. "It's not working anymore."

"Your TV's not working?" he asked Carol.

"It's not, and I don't know what the problem is. I've spent hours on the phone trying to fix the box, and CRC said they can't come until Friday. But that's our problem, not yours. Right, Marianne?"

Jim held up his hand and smiled. "No, it's fine Carol, I'll take a look. Let me get my stuff out of the truck."

"Yay! Thank you," Marianne said, hugging his leg.

He patted her on the head before she skipped back towards her mother.

"I really appreciate this, Jim," Carol said. "She's been driving me nuts ever since it went out yesterday." Jim opened the back door of the van, put some tools and wires in his work bag and closed the door as he followed behind them.

"So how are things?" Carol asked.

He sighed. "Alright, I guess."

"You guess?" she asked. Marianne bounded up the steps and ran inside as Carol held the door for him.

"Oh, it's nothing," he said. "Just, uh—"

"You had a fight with Sarah, didn't you?"

He nodded as he turned on the TV and pulled the cable box out. "How'd you know?" he asked, kneeling to work on the box.

"Because you haven't mentioned her yet," she said as she sat down on the couch to watch him work. Marianne sat down next to her mother and put her head in her lap.

"I don't always mention her," he protested and unhooked the box from the TV to run some new wire.

"Sure you don't," she said, sitting back on the couch and stroking Marianne's hair.

He finished screwing in the cables and flipped through the channels. A blue error message appeared on several of them.

Carol shook her head. "See, that's the same thing that happened to me. No one I called at CRC could figure out how to get rid of it."

"It's not that big of a deal, actually," he said. "Can I use your phone?"

"Sure," she said. Carol took the silver handheld phone from the end table and handed it to him.

He dialed his dispatch office, bracing himself for who was sure to answer.

"CRC Dispatch, this is Catherine."

"Hi Catherine, it's Jim."

"Hold on a second," Catherine said. "Hey, everybody, gather round, I got a real live superstar on the phone! Oh, this is the happiest day of my life."

"Alright, knock it off. I'm doing some work for—"

"You aren't working today, superstar, I damn sure know that."

"I'm trying to help a neighbor out," he said. "Can you bring up the Carol Michelson account at 711 Sugartown Road in Springfield?"

"I ain't pulling that up. You know you're supposed to call customer—"

"Catherine, please, she's a friend of Sarah's." Catherine harrumphed, but he heard her typing to bring up the information.

"What package do you have?" he asked Carol as he covered the phone with his hand.

"Mega HD," she said. "I think. I'm not sure, it was part of the promotion they ran in December."

"Alright, I've got her account up," Catherine said. "Now what?"

Jim ignored Catherine for a moment. "So you got a computer or gift card for free?" he asked Carol.

"The computer," Carol said. "But what's that—"

He held up his hand and nodded. "Alright, Catherine, can you change her package to the one listed under the ZFR4 code and then send a test signal?"

"What in the hell are you talking about? We haven't used that code in months," Catherine said.

"I know, but it's the same package, and I saw that e-mail a few months ago where you can change it to the old code, reset the signal, and change it back to the new one. It should fix the error code but not screw up billing."

"This I've got to see," Catherine said as she followed his instructions.

The box turned off and turned back on as Jim looked down at Marianne and winked.

"Alright, it's done," Catherine said.

Jim flipped through Carol's channels, and the error message was gone.

"Elmo's back!" Marianne yelled.

Catherine laughed over the phone. "Well, I'll be damned. Maybe you are a superstar," Catherine said.

"Yep, Knox the Superstar," Jim said, smiling at Marianne as he spoke. "Seriously though, thanks for the help."

"Anything for Miss Sarah. Besides, now that you're going to be working for me—"

"What?!"

"That's right, I guess the superstar didn't hear the news," she said. "I'd told CRC awhile ago if anything opened up I was looking to make the jump to manager, and thanks to you superstar, my ship has come in."

"Oh God," he said.

"No need for that. You can still call me Catherine," she said, cackling. "Or boss will work too. See you on Thursday, superstar!"

He sighed and tossed the phone back to Carol, shaking his head. "Everything okay?" Carol asked.

"Yeah, peachy," he said.

"Thank you, Mr. Jim," Marianne said, jumping off the couch and hugging his leg. He clapped his hands together like a blackjack dealer.

"You bet, Marianne."

"I can't thank you enough, Jim," Carol said, picking up the remote and flipping back to PBS Kids so her daughter could watch *Sesame Street*. "If you ever need anything, really." Marianne pulled a small play mat over from her toy corner and sat cross-legged on it in front of the TV.

"No worries," Jim said. He knelt down on the carpet to re-tie his shoes, stopping as he made the first loop. "Actually, I do have a favor to ask," he said.

"Sure, just name it," she said.

"Remember my buddy I was telling you about last week?"

"That guy you call Yeti?"

"Yeah, that's the one. I was going to ask if you wanted to come over on Saturday and meet him."

"Is he cute?"

"Depends if you think a hairy, mythological creature is cute. If you do, he's a god."

"I do like hairy chests," she said as she sat down in her rocking chair. "What does he do for a living?"

"He's a sales rep for a snack food company," he said, taking a seat on the couch. "He sells soft pretzels, water ice, that type of stuff."

"Soft pretzels? They're my favorite!" Marianne said. "I like Mr. Yeti, mommy."

"C'mon, it'll be fun," Jim said. "We were going to watch *Red Dawn* and make fun of Yeti trying to act cool in front of you."

She laughed and nodded. "I should be able to, but it depends on whether I can get any extra shifts down at Halo's this weekend." Halo's Diner was a neighborhood eatery within walking distance of the townhomes. He knew she'd been looking for something full-time ever since she'd been laid off from her customer service job with *TV Guide* several months earlier. "Is Sarah okay with me coming over?"

"Absolutely," he said, scratching the back of his neck. "Why wouldn't she be?"

Carol laughed at him. "You're a terrible liar. If Sarah's not comfortable with it, I'm not coming over."

"She hasn't said no, she just hasn't said yes yet, either."

"That's not why you were fighting today, was it?"

He shook his head. "No, we were fighting about Kit Kat bars."

"What?"

"Nothing, don't worry about it. I'm just considering a job offer down in Texas and—"

"You're not moving, are you Mr. Jim?" Marianne asked, leaning back on her mat and making a sad face at him.

"Marianne, stop." Carol pointed at the TV. "Just watch your show. Mr. Jim and I are talking. Jim, why would you ever want to work in Texas when you have a job right here you love and a wife who absolutely adores you?"

"I don't love my job," he said, stretching and shaking his head. "And I don't think Sarah 'adores' me."

"Jim, I've seen you two together. Wasn't it last Friday you two were out for a walk after work?"

"I guess. So?"

"Marianne and I were outside playing when you walked by. Sarah looked so happy she was with her guy on a beautiful Friday night. And not just happy, but proud of the guy she was with. You don't just give up something like that, especially when you love the job you have already."

"Why does everyone think I love my job? I'm so sick of people saying that."

She tapped her finger on the arm of her chair as she spoke. "Every time Marianne stops to talk to you about that van and splitters or cables or whatever, you look like you've won the lottery."

He shrugged. "Well it's important stuff."

"To you it is, because it's your job and you love it, no matter how much you try to deny it. And what's more, you're great at it. Look at what you just did in the other room. You fixed something in five minutes your entire company couldn't solve after the hours I spent on the phone with them."

"It doesn't matter, Carol. Maybe I do like it. But I'm not supposed to do this for the rest of my life," he said. "I'm just not."

"I wasn't supposed to get pregnant during a sorority mixer," she said, watching Marianne giggling and kicking her feet as Elmo played a piano on the TV screen. "But I wouldn't change a thing."

He half-smiled as he turned towards Marianne. "You're pretty persuasive. You should be a lawyer or something."

"I wish. I'd take anything that has a regular paycheck and benefits at this point," she said.

"Hmm."

"Hmm what?" she asked.

He pulled his wallet out of his front pocket and undid the Velcro to open it. He took out Cal's card. "Do you know who Cal Nolan is?"

"Of course."

"Well I did him a favor on Sunday, and he told me he was looking to hire a Knockout—"

"Don't do this," she said.

"Huh?"

"This is a gag, right?"

"A gag?"

"Someone told you I've been trying to get a job there, didn't they? I've sent my resume and headshot there ten times."

"No one tells me anything," he said. "But if you really do want that job, he told me to be on the lookout for someone and give them this." He handed her the card, and she cradled it in her hands.

"This isn't a trick then?"

"Nope. It's his private number. Just tell him I said you were knockout worthy."

"Jim, I don't know what to say."

"I'm quite something, I know."

"God, if I can get a job there, it would just be incredible. He offers medical, dental, child care discount, 401k, you name it. Should I call him now?" she asked, getting up out of her chair.

"I guess."

Carol dialed the number and put the phone up to her ear. "Yes, hi, is this Mr. Nolan?" Carol asked, fixing her hair while she spoke. "Hi, my name is Carol Michelson and Jim Knox asked me to call you and tell you he thinks I'm knockout worthy. Mmmhmm. I'm twenty-five. No, I've sent them already before. Tonight? Oh, that's wonderful, thank you so much. Yes, he's right here, hold on."

Carol could barely contain her excitement as she waved the phone at Jim. "He wants to interview me tonight! Oh, Jim, I can't thank you enough." She tossed him the phone. "Here, he wants to talk to you."

He bobbled the handset but made the catch. Carol scooped up Marianne in her arms and danced around with her as they covered their mouths from laughing too loudly while Jim was on the phone. "Hi, Cal," he said, putting his hand over his free ear.

"Hey Jim. We need to talk about something that happened today."

*   *   *

Sarah slammed the door behind her and threw her purse on the kitchen table. It was close to 2:30, and Jim's van was still sitting in the driveway, but he'd never returned her voicemail. She took her suit jacket off and hung it on the back of the kitchen chair before she rummaged through the liquor cabinet. The only thing they had was a half-empty bottle of cheap tequila Jim had brought home from a friend's bachelor party in Atlantic City.

She grabbed it and went to the refrigerator to mix it with something, but her only mixer option was the last bottle of Yoo-Hoo she'd turned down the day before. She wasn't about to drink terrible tequila straight, so she pulled out the Yoo-Hoo and brought both bottles to the sofa. Sarah cracked open the Yoo-Hoo and took a sip, then poured in as much tequila as she could before finally choking the mixture down. The house phone rang as her stomach groaned, and she set the bottle down to answer it without checking the caller ID.

"Hello?" she said, still smacking her lips from the aftertaste in her mouth.

"Is he home yet?" Charlotte asked. The women had spoken earlier after Sarah had tried to reach Jim repeatedly with no success.

"No, and I don't know where he is. He's still ignoring my calls," she said.

"You should be the one ignoring his calls. I can't believe he said that stuff to you."

"He was—" she stopped as the door from the garage opened and Jim threw his jacket on the table.

"He's home. I gotta go," she said. She put the phone back in the charger as she made eye contact with Jim for a moment before he looked at the tequila and Yoo-Hoo bottles on the table.

"Gringo Moreno, huh?" he said, coming into the living room and picking up the tequila bottle and shaking his head. "Never thought I'd see the day."

"If you don't mind, I'm not finished with that yet," she said. "And I can't believe you have a name for this stupid drink."

"Wait, was that the last bottle of Yoo-Hoo?" he asked as he set the tequila bottle down.

"Yeah, maybe you'll actually have to go to the store now," she said. "Don't you even want to know why I'm home?"

"Does it have anything to do with your little adventure at Scanlon's today Cal told me about?"

She picked up the Yoo-Hoo bottle and took another drink, her entire face puckering as it went down.

"That's what I figured. And since you're drinking the last bottle, maybe you should be the one who goes."

"Oh you want your wife to drive drunk and kill herself to get you some more Yoo-Hoo because you can't handle the one job around here I ask you to do?"

"No, I want my wife to go upstairs, sleep it off, and then go get me some Yoo-Hoo. And I just helped rake the leaves on Saturday!"

"Well whoop-de-doo," she said, taking a long sip this time. She wiped her mouth with her sleeve and pointed in the kitchen. "When you feel like actually keeping your promise to me, you know where to find the list."

He bit his lip and picked up the remote as he sat down in the recliner. "Whatever, I'm watching that Ford thing right now."

"No, you're not. I was here first."

"What are you, four?" he asked.

"This from the man who drinks Yoo-Hoo!" she said, shaking the bottle at him.

"No, this from the man who wishes he was drinking Yoo-Hoo!"

"Perhaps if you'd called me back and apologized for what you said earlier—"

"Oh, I have to apologize for what I said?" he asked, tapping his chest with his hand. "Why don't you apologize to me?"

"I already told you that you won in my voicemail."

"Well, I didn't get your voicemail because my phone was broken. But boy, I can't wait to post that on Facebook."

She folded her arms and slid into the corner of the sofa. "You would too, wouldn't you? Humiliate your wife like that. And how'd you talk to Cal if your phone was broken?"

"I was over at Carol's fixing her cable. She called him about a job, and he asked to chat with me."

"Just had to go over there, didn't you? After what you said to me—"

"I was doing my job. You know, that job you desperately want me to keep. Man, at least in Texas I wouldn't have to put up with stupid shit like this."

"Fine, go! Go to Texas, work for Cal, sleep with some bimbo. I don't fucking care, but leave me the hell alone."

"With pleasure." He got up and threw the remote control into the opposite end of the couch. It bounced off the sofa and skidded across the hardwood floor. Jim took the laptop and headed up the stairs.

Sarah heard the bedroom door slam shut as she finished the rest of her drink. She took her shoes off and lay back down on the couch. She closed her eyes and ignored the pains in her stomach as she lay there. It took only a few minutes before she fell asleep.

Jim's yell from upstairs awakened her from her nap. She shot off the couch and ran upstairs, flinging open the bedroom door. There she found Jim sitting on the bed in a *Karate Kid* t-shirt and boxers, the laptop resting on a pillow on his lap. She rubbed her eyes and looked around. "What's the matter? What happened?"

"What happened? ChakaKhan730 just kicked me out of Brazil, that's what happened."

She lowered her head and sat down on the edge of the bed, still blinking her eyes to wake herself up. "That's all?"

"I feel my troops pain," he said.

"You know what? Give me that," she said and took the computer from him. "I'm so sick of you losing to this woman."

"I actually think it's a guy."

"I don't care who it is. Now look, you've got all your troops sitting up here in Iceland and Ontario. You need to be more aggressive." She pointed at the board and then clicked through his turn, taking over almost all of Europe and North America.

"Wow, how'd you do that?" he asked, looking at his suddenly powerful empire on the virtual board.

"I don't know, I just saw how many troops you could get by turning in your cards this turn and figured out where Chaka was weakest and calculated—"

"I got it, Sarah," he said, chuckling. "I got it. I should have had you helping me all along."

She smiled and played with a loose thread on the comforter. "I'd like that," she said. "So Cal told you what happened earlier, huh?"

"Yep, told me about Karen and Bob and, well, you being offbase. I listened to my messages online a little while ago, too. That one you left is a keeper."

She set the laptop down on the bed and placed her hand on his leg. "Jimmy, I'm so sorry about what I said earlier. I didn't mean any of it. I just want you to be happy, and if that means you work in Texas or with Cal, I'll support whatever you want to do."

"Is that so?" he asked, folding his arms. "You won't give me grief or say I told you so the first time I have a rough day, and I'm complaining about how things are going?"

"I'll try my hardest not to, I promise."

He stared at her and frowned as he picked up his wallet from the bedside table. Pulling out a small piece of paper and unfolding it, he picked up the phone sitting on the bed next to him and dialed. He hit the speaker button and placed it on the pillow on his lap. "Well that makes my decision much easier then," he told her as the other end rang.

"Jim," Cal said. "I thought you weren't going to call back until tomorrow."

"Yeah, I know," he said. "I just thought it over and didn't think it made sense to wait. You see, I've got this other job lined up and—"

Her heart sank as she realized Jim was taking the job in Texas, but she bit her lip, so he wouldn't see her disappointment.

"It's Hollywood, isn't it? She's still holding you back even after her detective crap from today."

"No, it's not her, it's this—"

"Oh, give me a break," Cal said. "I used to see this all the time with my old man. He could have had everything I have, but he held back and ran every business decision by my mother. Spent his whole life worrying more about her happiness than his, and he just wasted his life. Don't make the same mistake he did."

"Cal, I really do appreciate what you did getting me all set up, but, I think this other job is a better career path for me, that's all."

"Jim, I know potential when I see it. You've got it, my friend. And no woman is worth it if she's holding you back from that."

She leaned over and hit mute on the phone. "Please, Jimmy, take this job. I don't want you to go to Texas. Please."

He waved her off and unmuted the phone. "I'm sorry, Cal. I know you pulled some serious strings for me, but there's another job I want more right now."

Cal sighed heavily over the speakerphone before responding. "I really thought you'd do the right thing for yourself here, Jim, I really did. At least let me give you a referral bonus for that sexy little squaw you sent my way. I pulled her picture from our files, and man oh man, I don't know how I missed Hiawatha before. Unless Hollywood won't let you take that, either?"

Jim looked up at her, and she forced a smile.

"No, that's very thoughtful. I know Carol will be great. She's very excited about meeting you."

"Alright then. I'll have a check down here at the office for you. Come by whenever to pick it up so that I can thank you again in person."

"I'll try and stop by tomorrow, if that's alright. I'm going to be busy later this week."

"Fine, I'll be here all day. See you then." Cal hung up before Jim could thank him.

Jim took a deep breath and started dialing the phone again. "I already told CRC what I wanted to do," he said. "But Catherine was hoping to chat with you before I moved on. Do you mind?"

"That's fine," she said, trying to sound positive. "I'd like to say goodbye to her."

"CRC Dispatch, this is Catherine." Jim lay the phone back down on the bed.

"Hi Catherine, it's Sarah," she said. "Jim said you want to—"

"Miss Sarah! Oh, thank you so much for calling. What is that damn fool up to now?"

"I'm sure he knows what he's doing," she said, as she took his hand. "And I support—"

"Well I don't see how laying this on me now is making my life any easier. I got a lot of Derek's nonsense to clean up."

"What are you talking about?"

"Oh the superstar is too busy to tell you I'm the new sheriff down here?"

She sighed and tucked her legs under her on the bed. "No, we've had a pretty busy day and now that's he starting that new job—"

"He's not starting it yet. I still need to check his references."

"What?"

"Well just because he's a superstar doesn't mean he can put in for the full-time position and expect me to hire him on the spot. And the only reference he said he had was you."

Sarah stared into Jim's eyes.

He nodded and looked back into hers. "I love you, Sarah," he said. "And I'm sorry. I hope you can for—"

She took his head in her hands and kissed him. "I love you too, Jimmy," she said as she pulled away. "Always."

"That'll do," Catherine said. "You got the job, superstar. See you on Thursday." Her line clicked off.

"Thanks for the reference," he said, touching his forehead to Sarah's. "Does this mean you forgive me?" She smiled and nodded as they kissed several more times.

"Are you sure this is what you want?" she asked.

"Very sure," he said, pulling her closer. "I even had Catherine e-mail me the paperwork to sign."

"You know, speaking of paperwork," she said, running her finger up and down his chest, "Whatever happened to the whole 'Felines for Frederick's' program?"

"Oh, it was suspended due to lack of funding."

"That's too bad," she said. She leaned over and whispered, "Because I was really looking forward to filling out those forms."

"Yeah, I bet. Wait, what?" He looked at her, and his eyes grew bigger. "I can have the program up and running in no time."

"Well . . . we need to go get my sponges anyway. I think we can—"

"Hooray for Hollywood!" He almost knocked her off the bed as he jumped up to gather his clothes.

12

"I want the red one first, and then the black one," Jim said, pushing open the door to the master bedroom and placing the multiple bags from Frederick's on the bed. Sarah came in behind him smiling and carrying the kitten, stroking his fur with her right hand.

"Alright, calm down," she said, kicking her shoes off. "I thought you were going to have a heart attack while we waited to check out."

He ripped his shirt off and fumbled with his belt. "Well who writes a check for twelve dollars? Get with the times, black bra grandma."

"Jimmy, calm down," she said, kissing him on the nose. "I'm not going anywhere. We can play all night if you want. Here, why don't you take Mr. Whiskers, so I can get changed?" She handed Jim the orange striped cat.

"Can we at least come up with a name other than Mr. Whiskers?" he asked.

"What did you have in mind?" she asked and sat down next to him as she undid her blouse.

"The Devil."

"No, Mr. Whiskers isn't the devil, are you Mr. Whiskers?" she asked like a four-year-old and scratched the cat's head.

"Ugh. How about . . . Pussy Galore?"

"No!"

"Reggie Jackson?"

She giggled and kissed Jim's cheek. "Alright, I can live with that."

"That's good," he said. Reggie purred as Jim put him down on the bed. Sarah picked up the bags and pulled out the clothing boxes, stacking them by the bed. She pulled out the bag from the drug store and took it and the top box into the bathroom.

He finished stripping down to his boxers and fluffed the pillows several times on the bed. Sarah had a carefully scripted pre-sex routine for special occasions she went through and changing into the present he'd waited for delayed things even longer. The bedside clock read 6:00 p.m., and the seconds ticked slowly by as he waited for her. "Are you coming soon? I don't how much longer I can hold out," he said.

"Patience, Jimmy," she said through the closed door. "I want everything to be just so."

He tapped his hands on the bed. "It's not going to matter if you don't hurry up. I'll have to take matters into my own hands."

Reggie hopped onto the bed and meowed. Jim grabbed him and set him on the floor, groaning when the cat jumped right back up. He shooed him away and made faces, but the cat just purred and curled up against him. He sighed and picked the cat up, holding him in front of his face. "Look, Reg, I've been waiting eleven-and-a-half years for this moment. Can you just be cool?"

He fist-bumped Reggie and set him back down on the floor. The cat ran out of the room, and Jim breathed a sigh of relief. Finally, the door to the bathroom opened. Sarah came out wearing the red lingerie they'd picked out. Her hair was down, and she wore bright red lipstick. She walked towards him slowly in high heels and had a devilish grin on her face.

"The, uh, the red stockings were an excellent choice," he said, swallowing and taking slow breaths.

"So you like it?" she asked as she modeled it for him.

"Oh, I'm declaring 'Felines for Frederick's' a—" He was interrupted by the cat jumping back up on the bed and purring as he curled up right next to him. "I never thought I'd say this, but I hate you, Reggie Jackson," he said, and set the kitten back on the floor. The cat jumped back on the bed and took up the same position.

Sarah giggled and took the unwanted guest out of the room.

The house phone rang, and he closed his eyes. "Please don't answer it, please don't answer it, please don't answer it," he said, knowing full well Sarah always answered the phone if they were home.

"Hello?" Sarah asked, picking up the phone in the spare bedroom.

Jim thrashed about on the bed, kicking his feet and pounding his hands against the mattress.

"Yes, this is she. Oh hello, Mr. Flynn. You didn't need to call back personally about my inquiries yesterday, your assistant—"

There was a long pause as Sarah walked back into the room with the phone and gave Jim a dirty look.

Uh oh, he thought.

"And you're sure it was from this number? Can you hold on a moment?" She placed the phone up against her chest to mute the mouthpiece.

"Jim, would you happen to know anything about leaving a message on Doug Flynn's voicemail yesterday afternoon around four o'clock?"

"I can't think of anything off the top of my head," he said, not looking at her.

"So you didn't call and yell 'Eat it Mr. Met, we're World Fucking Champions' on his voicemail?"

"Now does that sound like something I would do?"

She nodded vigorously.

"Well we are!"

She sighed in frustration and went back to the phone. "Yes, that was my husband, and he's very sorry. He wants to apologize to you personally about it." She put the phone on speaker and placed it on the bed. He snorted and leaned over towards the receiver.

"Yeah, it was just a little joke," said Jim.

"Is that so? You don't sound very sorry about it."

"Maybe I am Mr. Met, and maybe I'm not."

"You know, since you just did that work at my house, it might not look good for you as a technician, calling and harassing his customers. Might be something you get fired for."

"Oh god," Jim said, scratching his scalp and looking away from Sarah. "I didn't even think of that."

"Look, I'm a nice guy, and your wife was very pleasant to my assistant, so how about I just give you a 'Get Out Of Jail' free card instead?"

"You will?"

"Sure, I will. Just one little thing I'll need from you in return."

"An apology?" Jim asked, getting to his knees. "You got it. I'm sorry, I'm very sorry."

"No, I know you don't mean that. What I'll need is one very loud 'Let's Go Mets' from you. Then we'll be even."

"Never!" he said, picking up the handset and shouting in the phone. "I'll never say that. We can do a trade for something else, but not that. How about I try and roll doubles?"

"Sorry, but that's the only thing I'll take in return."

"No deal, Flynn. I will never—"

She leaned over and muted the phone. "Would you just make the trade? You're not really going to throw away your job just because you won't say 'Let's Go Mets', are you?"

"But, Sarah, I can't say 'Let's Go Mets'! I won't! I don't know how I'd live with myself, supporting those soulless—"

"Would you do it for me then? Please?" He looked at his wife in the lingerie and sighed, nodding his head.

"I'd do anything for you, Sarah." He kissed her forehead and unmuted the phone. "It's a deal."

"Okay, let's hear it then," Mr. Flynn said.

Jim sat up straight and took a deep breath. "Let's go Mets!"

"Ha, ha! That's the spirit."

"You may have won this round, Mr. Met, but—"

"Give me that," Sarah said, as he buried his head in a pillow and pretended to sob. She sat down next to him on the edge of the bed and adjusted her negligee.

"I'm sorry about that, Mr. Flynn," she said. "My husband can be so childish sometimes."

"No, hey, making a Phillies fan say that made it all worth it. If there's ever anything else you need from my office, please don't hesitate to call."

"I will. And I think it's wonderful what you're doing to help the Nolans keep Karen safe."

"Well, I appreciate that, thank you. But Cal did the hard part, I just happened to have the right house for Karen's situation. I'm sure she's glad it's all over."

"All over?"

"Of course. Now that Bob's dead, she can move out of there."

She gasped, and Jim popped his head up from the pillow. "When did this happen?" she asked.

"He died a few weeks ago. Some accident up in Delaware I think."

"Why that—" she said, shooting up off the bed. Sarah stopped and looked at Jim, smiling before she continued. "I'm just glad Karen is safe."

"So am I. Hey, I have to run, but if Jim needs any Mets tickets or anything, please let me know."

"Thank you so much, Mr. Flynn. Goodbye."

Jim arched his eyebrow as he sat up on the edge of the bed and looked at her. "Aren't you furious Cal lied to you?" he asked.

"What do you think?" she asked as she hung up the phone. "Of course I'm pissed. But what difference does it make? The bet's over."

"I know, but from what you told me earlier—"

"I broke a date with you because of Cal Nolan today already," she said, sitting on his lap and wrapping her arms around him. "And I'm never doing that again."

"Boy, that's a relief. I was sure you were going to ask me to snoop around his office tomorrow when I go to pick up that check."

"Well," she said, dancing her nails across his chest. "Now that you mention it, I wouldn't mind if you played Shaggy tomorrow for me."

"You wouldn't, huh?" he asked, chuckling.

She ran her hand through his hair and kissed him. "And if you ripped that cheesy moustache right off his smug little face, I wouldn't mind that either."

He laughed and kissed her. "Why don't I just poke around for now? But we can't be Velma and Shaggy. It's too weird, the idea of them sleeping together. "

"But I liked being Velma," she whined.

"Oh! We can be the Fords instead!"

She laughed and rested her head against his chest. "You're crazy."

"Aw, it'll be fun. I'll be Gerald."

"They weren't even detectives," she said, leaning back and looking at him.

"I know," he said and brushed her hair out of her face, "But they were great partners."

"They were, weren't they?" she said and put her head on his chest again. "Alright, Mr. President. I'm in."

"Hail to the chief, baby." They kissed, keeping their lips locked as they fell back onto the bed.

* * *

It was just after eight o'clock on Wednesday morning when they arrived at Philadelphia Hospital. Visiting hours didn't start for another half hour, but Sarah wanted to make sure everything was set for the conference call Mr. Donald had with Mr. Kim, who was traveling overseas. Jim had offered to drive the cable van so that he could park in one of the front spots reserved for maintenance vehicles to help Sarah with two large boxes of material she needed to bring. They sat in an almost empty waiting room, save for a few patients walking through on their way to the ER.

"Man, these magazines stink," he said, fiddling with his tie. "Look at these—*Highlights, Parents, Ladies Home Journal?*" She'd insisted he dress nicely today since he'd finally meet Mr. Donald when he helped her bring up the boxes before her conference call.

She looked up from her yellow legal pad and searched around her seat. "There's a *Readers Digest* and a *People* magazine sitting over here. You want one of those?"

"No, forget it. Is there anything you need help with?"

"I'm good, thanks," she said and smiled at him.

He drummed his fingers on the arm of the chair and watched her making notes. She tapped the floor as she wrote, and he smirked when he noticed her choice of footwear.

"I like your shoes," he said, pointing at them.

"Thank you," she said, not looking up from her work. "My husband got them for me."

"You're married?"

"Mmmhmm."

"What's he do?"

"Me." She didn't look up from her work but gave a sly grin, and the deadpan delivery caused him to burst out laughing, startling the woman at the front desk. He picked up the copy of *Ladies Home Journal.* One of the elevators along the wall to their left opened and a man hustled off. He slammed his hand on the desk and yelled, "When is somebody coming to fix the goddamn cable upstairs? I've been waiting for over an hour!"

"Please, Mr. Feeley, someone will be along soon," the receptionist said. "We've been having some problems—"

"Oh give it a rest. All you people ever give me are excuses why you can't do things. I just want something to work for once in this place."

The man kicked the desk and walked back to the elevators. He hung his head and pushed the call button, holding the bridge of his nose while he waited.

"Why don't you help him?" Sarah asked Jim. "We've still got awhile to wait."

"I don't know," he said. "He looks pretty mad. What about the boxes?"

"It's fine. If you're not back in time, I'll figure something out."

"Well if you can just figure something out, why'd I have to come down in first place?"

Sarah called across the waiting room. "Excuse me, sir? My husband Jim can help you out. He works for the cable company." The man from the elevator turned, and she pointed at Jim.

The man snorted and made a dismissive sweep of his hand.

"I don't need some suit to give me a credit for ten dollars off HBO," he said and entered the elevator.

"Hey, I'm no suit!" Jim yelled as the elevator doors closed. He went over to the reception desk and showed the woman his technician's ID from his wallet. "So what's that guy's problem?"

"His son is dying," she said. Jim's face turned bright red as she handed him the sign-in sheet and he scribbled his name. "The Feeleys are up in the ICU on the fourth floor, room eight. Just turn right off the elevators and they're at the end of the hall."

He thanked her and jogged out to his truck to get his gear. He took the elevator to the fourth floor and found the walls going to the ICU lined with inspirational cards and notes, all dedicated to the miraculous recovery of Michele Groves. There were several donation thermometers showing totals reaching three to four times what various charities were hoping to collect, and he smiled at the many pictures of children, all photographed as they were being discharged from the hospital.

The Feeleys were seated around a table eating some breakfast, save for their youngest son who was in a modified hospital crib with several machines surrounding it. A man and woman, both in their late twenties, and another boy who couldn't have been more than four, ate Honey Nut Cheerios.

"Look Daddy, it's Mr. TV!" the boy yelled, seeing CRC's logo on Jim's bag as he went to knock on the door.

"Don't point, Peter, it's not polite," his father admonished him. Mr. Feeley wiped his mouth and came over to greet Jim. "I am so sorry, I didn't know. I just saw the tie and—"

"No worries," Jim said, "I'm Jim, by the way."

"I'm Adam," he said as they shook hands. "This is my wife Niamh, my son Peter, and that's Chris sleeping." Niamh's face was puffy and red. A mountain of literature sat next to her cereal bowl.

"Let's see what the problem is," Jim said. He set his gear down by the window and looked behind the TV. The line running from the TV into the wall was frayed, and he knew he'd have to replace the entire line for the signal to come back. "I can fix this no sweat, but it's going to take about twenty minutes. I'll try and stay out of your way."

"Thanks, I appreciate it," Adam said. "Peter here has wanted to watch *Bob the Builder* all morning."

"Hey, me too," Jim said, smiling at Peter, who clapped and bounced in his chair. Jim took out his tools, crouching down to remove the cable from the outlet.

A woman knocked on the open door. "Hello? Mr. and Mrs. Feeley?" Adam waved the heavyset woman into the room.

"Hi, I'm Brianna Spencer. I'm the case worker that's been assigned to Chris. Is this a good time to go over some things?" she asked, looking at Jim and then at the Feeleys.

"No problem, I can step out," Jim said. He stood before putting his tools back in the bag. Adam shook his head and motioned for him to stay put.

"Please, stay," he said.

"Are you sure?" Jim asked.

"It's fine. I just want it fixed."

"Alright, your call." Jim went back to work as Niamh pulled a chair out for the woman who sat down and opened a large folder. Peter sat on a small mat in the corner and played with his trucks.

"I wanted to spend some time talking about some of the expectations now that Chris has been diagnosed with SMA," she said, her voice steady and calm. "This list talks about some of the changes you should be on the lookout for over the next few months." She slid it in front of them, pausing a few moments before continuing. "You're going to notice a rapid decrease in Chris's motor functions. He'll be unable to move any of his extremities at all within three to six months, possibly sooner."

Jim tried to concentrate on his work as the woman spoke, but he heard Niamh sniffle when he glanced at her. She held Adam's hand and wiped her eyes.

"It's also very important you keep him away from anyone who might be sick. His immune system is already breaking down and any small virus could kill him. Keep a supply of hand sanitizer in every room of the house, along with whichever car will have his special car seat. I wouldn't recommend taking him out unless absolutely necessary, however."

"Well I'm not having my kid turn into a goddamn bubble boy," Adam said.

"It's just a suggestion, but you'll find travel difficult. If you need to take him somewhere, you'll need all the same equipment you have for him at home to be prepared for any contingency. Oxygen tanks, suction machines, nebulizers, etc."

"Oh, Chris," Niamh said.

"Once you've done it a few times, it'll become easier, but you must have everything you'd have at home for him available at all times," Brianna said. "Even the smallest infection could go to his lungs and require immediate hospitalization or even bring upon complete respiratory failure."

"So what are we supposed to do?" Adam asked, locking his hands around the back of his neck. "I've got to travel for work. I can't be home to help load Chris and all that stuff in the car every time we need milk."

"I understand, although you might consider taking some time off—"

"We can't afford that! I don't know how I'm going to pay for this stuff anyway," he said and picked up the list. "I mean, I don't even know what a Pulse Oximeter is, and it's fifteen thousand dollars."

"Don't worry about the cost. All of these items are covered by the state and grants from the Michele Groves foundation. You're very lucky to -"

"Did you just call us lucky?" Niamh asked. "I was told twelve hours ago my baby boy is going to die, and you tell me how lucky I am? Get out of my son's room."

Brianna backpedaled from her clumsy remark. "I'm sorry, I just—"

Niamh stood up and screamed at the woman. "Get out of here now!" Her shrill voice pierced the silent hallways of the ICU. Brianna left the folder and walked out of the room, shutting the door behind her to avoid any further escalation. Chris awoke after hearing his mother's outburst and cried.

"Oh, Chris sweetie, calm down. Mommy's sorry," Niamh said. Jim stole another glance at Niamh, as she pulled her chair next to the bed. She hummed a lullaby as she stroked Chris's face with the back of her hand.

"I'm sorry about that," Adam said to Jim before going to his wife and caressing her shoulders as they looked at their son.

"It's fine, I'm just about done," Jim said. He took another minute and screwed the cable back into the TV before Peter tugged on his shirt to see what he was doing.

"What's up, buddy?" Jim asked.

"Mr. TV, when you're done fixing that, can you please fix my brother?" he asked Jim.

Jim turned and looked at him, giving him a sad half-smile. "I wish I could, buddy," he said and patted the boy's head, fighting the lump forming in his throat. "But I'll tell you what I can do." He rose to his feet and clicked on the set. *Bob the Builder* appeared on the screen.

"Yay, Bob!" Peter said, and slapped Jim's outstretched hand before returning to his chair. Jim gathered his gear and looked at the scene by Chris's bed, seeing the mask and tube that covered much of Chris's tiny face. He slipped out of the room as Adam gave him a slight nod goodbye.

Jim slouched against the side of the elevator as he rode down, stepping off slowly upon reaching the lobby. He walked over to Sarah and stood in front of her as she gathered up her things.

"Perfect timing," she said, "I was just about to try and find someone to help me bring these up."

"Do we have to go up now?" he asked. She looked at her watch and shrugged.

"Well, it's almost 8:30. I guess you have a couple minutes if you want to—Jimmy, what's the matter?" she asked.

"Just walk with me out the van," he said, taking her hand.

"I don't have much time—"

"Please, Sarah."

"But I can't just leave—"

"Please."

She smiled and nodded, and he laced his fingers with hers as they headed out the door together.

13

It was just after 10:30 a.m. when Jim stood in front of the Nolan Realty office. He'd left Sarah back at the hospital shortly before nine and had stopped to get a new phone. She had promised to call as soon as her meeting was finished to see if they could meet for lunch.

He opened the door to the main entrance. Nolan Realty had taken over the first two floors of the building located only minutes from City Hall. From the wall of good deeds showing off Cal's involvement in various charity endeavors to the blonde cleavage-bearing receptionist who smiled broadly when she saw Jim come in, the stamp of Cal was everywhere.

"Welcome to Nolan Realty. Do you have an appointment scheduled with a Knockout?"

"Yeah, but not till I pick her up later," he said. "I'm actually here for a check that Mr. Nolan has for me."

"Oh, you must be Mr. Knox," she said. "Mr. Nolan is expecting you. Have a seat and I'll call—" She stopped speaking when Cal stepped off the elevator at the back of the lobby and hurried towards the front entrance.

"Just couldn't let it go," Cal muttered, oblivious to Jim's presence as he walked by.

"Mr. Nolan, Mr. Nolan," the receptionist called to Cal as he breezed by. "Mr. Knox is here to see you."

Cal glanced over at the desk and came over to shake Jim's hand. "Sorry, Jim didn't recognize you there. You haven't changed your mind about that job I suppose? It isn't too late."

"I appreciate that, thank you, but I'm all set," Jim said. "How did Carol's interview go?"

"Fantastic. I hired her on the spot. Look, I have to jet. Ms. Tedesco, please take Mr. Knox up to my office and grab the check off my desk for him. He might enjoy seeing how the other half lives."

"Yes, Mr. Nolan," she said.

"Best of luck, Jim. And don't let Hollywood wear the pants in your marriage all the time. Be a shame to cover those gams up." He patted Jim on the shoulder and headed out the door. *You got that right*, Jim thought.

"If you'll follow me please." Ms. Tedesco smiled and beckoned Jim onto the elevator. They went up one floor and walked down the hallway towards the double-doors of his private office. She fumbled with the key in the door.

"He doesn't have a private secretary or four?" he asked.

"No, he thinks they're a waste of money," she said and opened the door. "He takes care of his own scheduling."

Cal's office was the size of half a football field. It was one of the most impressive rooms Jim had ever stepped in, with two large glass conference tables and several murals adorning the walls along with a headshot of every one of his "Knockouts." On the wall behind the large mahogany desk, there were pictures of various political figures, including shots with the governor, the mayor and various members of congress all surrounding a large plasma TV.

Jim walked behind the desk as Ms. Tedesco finished thumbing through one pile of envelopes and picked up another. The desk had three computer screens and several photos of his wife and son. He spotted a Frederick's of Hollywood catalog in a pile of mail next to the phone with a rubber band around it. He tried to slide it closer to him without the secretary noticing.

On one of the envelopes bundled with it, there was a small note on it that read—"Karen—11 at Philly Hosp." The time on the multi-line desk phone showed it was 10:43.

"What do you think you're doing?" she asked as she stuck the envelope with his check in front of his face.

"I just, uh, saw the catalog and—"

"I don't care what you saw. That's today's mail, and you shouldn't be touching it. I think it's time for you to go." She handed him the envelope, and they rode down the elevator in uncomfortable silence.

"So, any chance for a hug?" he asked, as she escorted him to the front entrance. "You look like a hugger."

"Get out!" she said as he scrambled out the glass door.

*   *   *

Sarah stood in front of the bathroom mirror down the hall from Mr. Donald's room and checked her turquoise blouse and black skirt for any trace of the coffee she'd spilled on the floor coming back from the hospital cafeteria. Convinced she'd escaped any stains, she adjusted her hair and picked up her purse to call Jim when her phone beeped to signal a new text message.

"driiivng bak ther," it said. She dialed as fast as she could after she read it and Jim answered.

"Hi sweet—"

"Jimmy, quit texting and driving. You're going to kill somebody," she said.

"Sorry, wasn't sure if you were—" The line went dead as she looked at the phone and saw the call had been dropped. She got her purse and opened the door to try and call him back when her phone rang again.

"Why did you hang up?" she asked as a nurse frowned at her for being on a cell phone. She headed into the nearby stairwell to go down to the main lobby.

"Sorry, I'm still trying to program the hands-free device with this new phone," he said.

"And you're doing that while you're driving?"

"I'm using both knees to steer."

"Not funny," she said as she exited to the main level. "So what did you find out?"

"I think he's on his way to you. He's meeting Karen over there at eleven, or I think he is anyway."

As she made her way through the hallways back towards the main entrance, she checked the time on her phone. It was 10:46 a.m. "He told you this?"

"No, he was leaving when I got there. I saw the note about the meeting when the receptionist took me up to his office to get the check."

"And how did you convince her to do that exactly?"

"How do you think?"

"I'm guessing he ordered her to."

"Pretty much."

She chuckled and walked into the lobby to find it jammed with people. She headed outside to the entrance of the hospital.

"I had to go outside. The lobby is pretty crowded. Anyplace you think I should look for them out here?"

"Um, try waiting down at the bus stop we went past on Spruce. You can at least see the public parking lots from there. If you don't see him, I'll just pick you up, and we can circle back and grab those boxes you brought."

"Okay, sounds good. I have to be back at the office by 12:30," she said, making her way to the bus stop at the end of the block. "While I have you, I was hoping we could work out—"

Jim's line went dead. She sighed and sat down on the long white bench, watching Spruce Street for any sign of Karen or Cal. After five minutes of keeping vigil, she saw a blue Porsche in front of a black BMW. The BMW flashed its lights and honked while both cars sat in a solid line of traffic. Standing and walking to the edge of the curb, Sarah watched the blue Porsche turn into a small parking lot, and the black BMW followed behind.

"That's them," she said and called Jim as she crossed the street towards the private lot.

"The number you have reached is no longer in service," Jim said. "Please try—"

"Stop, I just saw Cal and Karen," she said, her heels clicking as she moved past the tow-away sign for the lot. "They pulled into the parking lot next to Myrtle's building. I'm heading in now."

"I don't want you doing anything crazy. I'll be back there in five or ten minutes. Wait for me."

"I just want to hear what they're saying."

"It's too dangerous. At least let me send the Secret Service."

"Would you quit it!" she said and crept along the parking lot by the side of the building and peered around the corner, spotting them about fifty feet in front of her. Cal banged on Karen's car door. "Alright, I see them. They've just parked in the back behind the building," Sarah said to Jim. "I can't believe how quiet this lot is. It's eerie."

"Baby, please be careful. I'm just worried—"

"I'll be fine," she whispered. "Can I record video on this phone?"

"Yeah, but you have to hang up with me."

"Just tell me what to do."

"Change the photo option in the menu and then hit start. There should be a blinking red button if it's working."

"Thanks. Get here as soon as you can, okay?"

"On my way, Betty!"

Sarah hung up and moved closer to Cal and Karen, crouching first behind a red sedan and then moving around the rear corner of the building, changing the options on her phone as she got within twenty feet. Behind a tan Honda Accord she held the camera up to zoom in. Cal still banged on the door when Karen finally stepped out, dressed in another expensive and revealing outfit.

"What the hell are you doing?" Cal asked.

Karen lifted the sunglasses off her eyes and said, "What does it look like I'm doing? I'm trying to find out where—"

Cal took Karen's arm as she leaned against the car. "Now you listen. I'm getting sick of telling you over and over that you can't go out until I have everything finalized. You keep getting these so-called ideas, and I'm stuck cleaning up the mess. Charging my account for new clothes, running a cable line to the garage to do pilates in the right light, and now coming down here to ask questions about the baby. I've made a big investment in you. Don't make me regret it."

She wrestled her arm free and poked him in the chest. "Don't you ever touch me like that again. That's what Bob used to do before—"

"I know damn well what Bob did. But he's gone now, and if you want us to be together—"

"But I want Jane back, Cal. That little story the *TODAY* show did about Michele was so sweet, and I was thinking we could have our own little family with Jane when you and I are finally together."

"Karen, she's gone. I took her to the hospital and gave her up, period. There are no refunds, and no way to get her back now, so quit trying. It's too late."

"Are you sure there's nothing you can do? You know a lot people, maybe you—"

"Not this time. She went from Jane Scanlon to Jane Doe the minute I dropped her off. So let it go, and stay out of sight until Friday like I told you, unless you want to stay in that crappy house forever."

"No, I don't," Karen said. "But I'm bored out there. I can only do pilates for so long—"

"And it's paying off. God, you turn me on." Cal grabbed Karen's thigh and squeezed hard. "This body is hotter than ever."

"Ohh! Calvin," she said, "I thought you were mad about my pilates."

"Not about the results," he said, kissing her hard as she reciprocated. "Trust me, baby. I've got the lawyers working overtime so I can fight that post-nup next month. But once I tie up a few loose ends, I can give you something Bob never did. I'll finally be able to start putting money into our very own joint account by Friday night. And I'm going to deliver the checks to you myself. It'll give us a chance to celebrate."

"I can't wait, Calvin. Alright, I'll see you on Friday." They kissed again, and she climbed back in her car as he smacked her ass. Karen backed the car out, blowing a kiss to him as she drove off. Sarah slumped back down in her hiding spot, her hands shaking. She balanced herself against the wall on her new heels, counting the seconds until Cal drove off as well.

She watched Cal grin and slide his sunglasses back on as Karen departed. He walked back to his BMW and his car beeped as he clicked his key to unlock the door. She took a small step towards him while still crouching to get a better view. One of her heels buckled, and she tumbled to the ground, dropping the phone.

Cal's head snapped around, and she held her breath as he moved slowly in her direction. She reached to corral the phone, trying not to make any noise as she watched his shiny wingtips move towards her. He stopped and listened as she pulled the phone back. There wasn't a movement or sound for a few seconds, but then Cal dropped to the ground to look under the cars, and their eyes locked. She frantically tried to get to her feet as Cal leapt to his. Realizing she couldn't outrun him, she sent the video to Jim and watched the send status meter slowly rise on the large file. It had only reached twenty-five percent when Cal pinned her against the wall and covered her mouth. He checked to make sure no one was coming. Satisfied they were alone, he shook his head as he looked at her.

"Don't make a sound," he said, removing his hand from her mouth and taking the phone from her hand. He looked at the video file that was still uploading and threw it against the ground, smashing it and stomping on it with his shoe for good measure.

"This isn't a game, Hollywood," he said, as she squirmed to free herself from his hands locked on both wrists. "I just want to be with the woman I love on my own terms," he growled, leaning right into her face. "And no one is going to wreck that for me. So drop the detective act and leave us alone. Do you understand me?"

"You don't tell me what to do," she said.

"Let's get something straight, Hollywood," he said, his hot breath stinging her eyes as he spoke. "I'm not Jim, and I never will be. Because unlike Jim, I'm not going to stay married to someone like you. A selfish, pushy, shrew of a woman, who cares more about herself than her marriage."

"That is not true," she said, shaking her head. "Let go of me, you son of a bitch."

"I'll let go, Hollywood," he said, releasing her wrists. "It's just too bad Jim won't."

"You don't know anything about me!"

"Sure I do, Holly—"

"My name is Sarah Knox, you ASSHOLE!" she screamed in his face.

He wiped her spittle from his cheeks. "Your name is meaningless to me, you stupid bitch."

He turned to walk back towards his car, and she ran to his driver's side door to block his path.

"Well guess what, Calvin?" she asked, tapping her long fingernails on the shiny exterior of the car. "Bitches get things done, and I'm going make sure Bonnie finds out about you and your little whore."

Cal shoved her out of the way, and she stumbled on her heel and fell to the ground. Her head clipped the bumper of his BMW, and she moaned in pain.

"You call her a whore again," he said and knelt down next to her. "And you'll get a lot worse than that. You're nothing compared to her. Nothing."

She touched her head to see if she was bleeding. "I'm going to—"

"Save it, we're done," he said. "I've got better things to do than this."

Sarah struggled to get to her feet and fell to one knee, still woozy from the bump on her head. "Yeah, like screwing that whore behind your wife's back!"

Cal stopped and marched towards her as she backed away. "Hollywood—" Sarah covered her head as he raised his hand, and then she heard a yell.

"No!" the old woman's voice yelled. Sarah recognized it as Myrtle's. A muscular man held Cal against the BMW, his fist poised to strike. "Don't hit him, Clarence," Myrtle said. "You're better than that."

Clarence nodded and relaxed his grip a bit.

Cal laughed at him as he did this. "Unbelievable. Even Yo-jimbo here gets pushed around by some wrinkly old prune. God doesn't anyone have balls except me anymore?"

Clarence cracked his knuckles and looked at Myrtle. She nodded her approval.

"Thanks, Myrt," Clarence said, grinning and punching Calvin in the stomach. Calvin moaned and slid to the ground, writhing in pain and trying to catch his breath.

Jim ran around the corner and saw Cal slump to the ground. He tore over to Sarah as she embraced him and steadied herself.

"What happened?" Jim asked. "What did that bastard do?"

"He shoved me into his car," she said, pointing at the BMW. "I bumped my head pretty good."

"You hurt her? You hurt my wife, you sonofabitch?" Jim asked. He moved towards Cal, but Sarah wouldn't let go.

"Goddammit, I had him, Jimmy. I had proof in my hands and that bastard smashed my phone," she said.

"Are you talking about that video?"

"What?"

"Yeah, I just got it from you a few minutes ago. That's why I called Myrtle to make sure you were okay when I couldn't reach you. Thank god she gave me that card."

"You mean it? You got the whole thing?"

He nodded. "It's guess. I only saw the begin—"

She smiled and hugged him. "Oh, thank you Jimmy. Thank you."

"Wow, it must be some video."

"That man needs to learn some manners," Myrtle said, shaking her head as Clarence kept a close watch. "Are you okay, Sarah?"

"I'm fine now, thanks to you both," she said, wiping her eyes.

"Oh, pish tosh. Go get yourself looked at over at the hospital. Clarence and I will clean up this mess." Clarence picked Cal up by his lapels and pushed him against the car. "Why don't we see if our new friend might be willing to do a little work around my office?" she asked.

"Good idea," Clarence said and dusted Cal off. "C'mon friend, I have a sign I could use your help with."

14

Jim sat next to the examination table and watched Sarah as an intern checked her eyes with a penlight. It was just after noon, and the Philadelphia police were supposed to arrive momentarily to take her statement. She sat up as the intern made some notes in his chart, and Sarah pulled her hair back into a ponytail. Jim stood and kissed her bump as she smiled.

"You'll be fine," the intern assured her. "Just a bump on the head, and there's no sign you suffered a concussion. You might have a little pain the next few days but nothing major. Would you like some aspirin?"

"No, thank you," Sarah said. "I'm feeling okay."

"Good, well, we're going to move you to a conference room for your discussion with the police. Follow me, please." Jim helped Sarah step down from the examination table and held her hand as they walked out of the busy ER and snaked through several hallways. Her steps were labored as she navigated the floors in her ruined heels.

She squeezed his hand as they entered the conference room. On the far wall was a large whiteboard and a TV cart with DVD player, and in the middle of the room stood an oval table with a phone on it. Jim pulled out one of the brown leather chairs for Sarah, and she sat down as he pushed the chair in for her. He sat next to her and spun around a few times until she grasped the handle to indicate play time was over.

"Can I watch the video again?"

"How many times are you going to watch that?" Jim asked as he handed the phone to her.

"I just want to make sure it's real," she said grinning as she watched Cal's rendezvous with Karen. "I still can't believe you got this from me."

"You realize the only thing that proves is he's having an affair. Dropping a baby at a hospital isn't a crime."

"I know," she said, continuing to watch.

"Then what happened to the whole that's between him and his wife and his conscience and that Samuel Johnson jazz from the diner?"

Sarah tilted her head towards him and frowned. "Fuck. That."

A knock on the door came as she finished the three minute replay, and Sarah handed the phone back to Jim. A police officer poked his head in and removed his hat.

"Sarah Knox?" he asked.

"That's me," she said. The officer nodded and closed the door behind him as he entered the room.

"I'm Officer Lou Etezady, with the Philadelphia police. Sorry it took so long. It's been a busy morning."

"Boy, there's a shock," Jim mumbled.

The officer shook their hands, sat down across from them, and set his small tape recorder and notepad on the table. "Okay, Mrs. Knox, we'll just take it nice and slow and let me know if you have any questions. I know you've been through a lot already, so I don't want to rush you."

"I'm ready, trust me," she said and folded her hands on the table.

"Can you say and spell your name please?"

"Sarah Knox, S-A-R-A-H K-N-O-X."

"And your age?"

"Thirty-five."

"Occupation?"

"Executive Assistant at Donald and Kim."

"Alright, so, this man who attacked you, this Clarence Yang, he—"

"What? Clarence didn't attack me, Cal Nolan did."

The officer stopped and checked his notes to confirm. He shook his head and tapped his pen on the table. "Nope, it was Clarence Yang."

Jim and Sarah looked at each other in disbelief.

"You think I don't know who attacked me?" she asked.

The officer leaned back in his chair and threw up his hands. "Well we already interviewed Mr. Nolan, and he told us what happened. This was just for corroboration."

"Corroboration? He hit my wife!" Jim said.

"That's not how Mr. Nolan tells it."

"Of course he doesn't tell it that way!" Sarah said. "You think he'd just come right out and confess?"

"Look, I—"

Another knock came at the door. The officer clicked off his tape recorder and walked over to open the door. A man's voice could be heard asking the officer to step outside. The officer obliged, closing the door to the conference room behind them.

"What was that all about?" Jim asked.

"Cal," she said, closing her eyes and shaking her head. "It has to be."

"Screw that. I don't care what happens, Cal's only getting this video when he queues it up on Netflix like everyone else."

The door re-opened and an older man appeared without the officer. As he closed the door, he walked to the table set down his briefcase.

"I'll just be a moment," the man said. He picked up the phone as they exchanged a confused glance at one another.

"You know who this old dud is?" Jim leaned over and whispered.

Sarah nodded. "I think it's Beth—"

"Yes, this is Judge Snyder. Can you connect me to the family's room my daughter is visiting? I believe their name is - Thank you." Sarah and Jim both now recognized him as Judge Francis Snyder, Beth's father, baby Michele's grandfather. He turned his back to them as he resumed the conversation. "Hello, Mr. Feeley? Yes, this is Judge Snyder. May I speak to my daughter please?"

"What the hell is he doing here?" Jim asked.

"I don't know," Sarah whispered back. "Maybe this affects the status of that discrimination lawsuit somehow."

"Hi Beth," the judge said, tugging at the skin on his cheek. "I'm here. I'll send someone up to escort you to the conference room. Are you sure this is what you want to do? Alright, I'll see you in a few minutes."

The judge hung up the phone and walked to the door. He poked his head out, then closed the door and took a seat a seat across from them. "I'm sorry about the confusion with the officer," he said, taking and setting his case by his feet. "I didn't expect Cal to call the police so quickly after speaking to me, but, well I guess you already know what that man is like. Do you both know who I am?"

"We do, but we don't understand why you're here," Sarah said.

"Right now I'm keeping you both safe. I'll explain everything as soon as Beth gets down here."

"Why do you need her here?" Jim asked.

"Judge, there's no one I admire more than Beth. And we're sorry for what she's been through, but I don't see why she needs—"

"Mrs. Knox, we'll explain everything as soon as she gets here, I promise. So please, just be patient. Can I get either of you something to drink?"

Jim sat up in his chair. "Actually, I'd take a Yoo—"

Sarah interrupted him. "We're fine, thanks." The three of them sat in an uncomfortable silence as they waited for Beth's arrival. Jim took Sarah's hand and fondled it gently with his thumb and forefinger. There was a knock on the door, and Beth entered carrying a sleeping Michele in her arms. Her father closed the door behind them, and Beth and her father sat down across from Jim and Sarah.

"I'd shake your hand, but I'm kind of tied up right now," Beth said. Michele wore a small pink dress that read "Fight SMA" on it, and Beth wore a matching pink t-shirt. "I understand you met the Feeleys earlier, Mr. Knox. Their little boy couldn't stop talking about the magic man who fixed the TV."

Jim chuckled and nodded. "Yeah, I'm a regular Blackstone."

"The name Jim Knox sounds familiar, too," she said. "Didn't you get arrested with a bunch of other kids trying to break into my sister's high school with some keys you'd stolen?"

"See, that's a misunderstanding. I was merely part of the pre-planning team that—"

"Jim, not now," Sarah said.

"Mr. and Mrs. Knox, we're here to ask a favor of you," the judge said. "We'd like you to destroy the video you have of Mr. Nolan."

Sarah folded her arms and shook her head. "No way. Absolutely not."

"Why on earth would we do that?" Jim asked him.

The judge took a deep breath and looked at his daughter. She kissed Michele's head and nodded to him. He wiped his brow and proceeded. "Three months ago, my daughter met with a man the night Michele probably would have died. He told her he was a doctor and had developed a procedure that would save Michele's life. For this procedure to work, however, he basically needed to suck the disease out of her."

"What? That's insane," Jim said.

"That's what I thought too," Beth said. "But in his office, he called someone and then showed me a video feed of Michele in her room. She started moving her arms and legs, and she was a normal baby for the first time in her life. It was wonderful."

"Who did he call?" Sarah asked.

Michele fidgeted in Beth's lap but didn't wake. "He called my late husband's number," she said. "Which I'd never had shut off. I'd just had it—"

"She had it forwarded to a prayer voicemail box," the judge interrupted.

"A prayer voice mailbox?" Sarah asked. "I don't understand."

"It's something Beth's church setup for people to leave messages of support for military families that lost loved ones. People kept calling Steve's phone to say how they were praying for her, so—"

"Look," Jim said, moving his chair closer to Sarah, "I really don't care if he called God or The Ghostbusters. I just want to know what this has to do with Cal Nolan assaulting my wife."

"We're getting to that," the judge said. "This doctor explained that for the procedure to work, he needed a host provided by another parent. This baby would then have the disease transferred to it from Michele. Once the procedure was over, Michele would be healthy, but the other baby would die."

"That's impossible," Sarah said.

"Show it to them, Daddy," Beth said.

Her father opened his briefcase. "Beth, I wish you would reconsider this," he said. "They're not going to understand."

"I have faith they will," she said and nodded at Jim and Sarah. The judge shook his head but obliged his daughter, opening the briefcase and pulling out a DVD. He took it out of the case and walked over to the TV cart, pausing for a moment before he powered on the system.

"The doctor who performed the procedure videotaped it for his files," he turned and told them. "He gave us a partial copy as well."

He slid the DVD into the tray. The picture came up and was focused on a door with a sign that read "Warning—Not A Fire Exit" on it. A man's arm pushed open the door and moved the camera through the doorway to reveal two children in basinets in an empty room with a blue and white checked tile floor and a door on the opposite wall with a crash bar.

"That's that darkroom in Myrtle's office," he whispered to her.

"What? Oh yeah, she mentioned that sign," Sarah said. "Odd looking darkroom."

One of the two babies was baby Michele, who had her eyes closed and a tube inserted into her arm. The second baby looked to be a newborn and was crying. The tube from Michele ran directly into the second child's chest. A man's back came into the frame and blocked the camera view for a moment. After he moved away, Michele's eyes were wide open and her arms and legs kicked. There was a greenish liquid moving through the tube and entering the chest of the second child. The newborn screamed, and her body appeared to get redder and redder, like she was rapidly getting sunburned. Blisters began appearing on her skin, and the screaming became more intense. The video cut out and the judge turned off the monitor.

"This is all we have," Beth explained with tears in her eyes. "He told us it's just meant to be his insurance policy."

"Oh god," Sarah said, motioning at the screen with an open right hand. "How could you do that?"

"I didn't plan to," Beth said, patting Michele's back and rocking her. "When I got back to the room that night, I talked to my father and prayed about it and decided not to go through with the procedure. I decided instead to commit my life to fighting this horrible disease and was just thankful my baby had a few healthy hours before I knew she would die."

"Except Michele's sitting right there in your lap," Jim said.

"Well, that's where Cal comes in," the judge said. "He was the host's father. He'd apparently been approached by the doctor to donate his baby. When Beth called back to say there was no deal, the doctor told Cal the deal was off. Cal then called Beth directly and said he was going to kill his baby and throw her in the trash, so Beth was letting Michele die for no good reason."

"Bullshit," Jim said. "Even Cal wouldn't do something like that."

Beth rocked Michele and rubbed her own left earlobe, her eyes on the floor. "When Cal told me that, it was enough to convince me. I signed the papers and agreed to the procedure. All Cal wanted in return for his baby was my father to dismiss the lawsuit against him. As soon as Daddy did that, Cal promised he'd make the full payment for the procedure."

"And you agreed to this?" Sarah asked the judge.

He pursed his lips and nodded once. "You'd be surprised what a father would do for his little girl," the judge said and clutched Beth's shoulder.

"That doesn't make it right!" Sarah said.

"You're right," the judge said. "It doesn't. But I love my daughter, and I love my granddaughter, and I'd do anything for them." He patted Beth's arm, and she looked back at them.

"My father is supposed to dismiss the lawsuit tomorrow," Beth said. "While Cal hasn't seen the video you just saw, he knows the doctor recorded the procedure, and that if payment isn't made within ninety days, the contract states the doctor can sell the video to the tabloid press or some nonsense and get the money that way."

"You're kidding," Jim said. "Miracle baby there might be on *Inside Edition* or something?"

"If that's the case, why did you wait so long to dismiss the lawsuit?" Sarah asked the judge.

"I wanted to make sure the plaintiffs wouldn't have enough money to continue on appeal," the judge explained. "And at this point, after all the hurdles Cal's put up for them, they won't. Their flimsy case will die once and for all."

"Just because you're crooked doesn't make their case flimsy," Sarah argued. "I can't believe this. You're actually asking us to help you cover up multiple crimes by destroying our video. We'd never do that."

"Yeah, screw you guys. Call the nutty doctor who did this and talk to him about your payment troubles," Jim said, getting up from his chair.

"We can't do that," Beth said.

"And why not exactly?" Sarah asked as she rose from her seat.

"Because he's dead," the judge said, opening his briefcase and pulling out a manila folder. "And has been for almost sixty years." They both stopped as the judge slid the folder across the table to them. "See for yourself."

Jim looked at the somber faces of Beth and her father as he picked up the folder and opened it. The top sheet was a printout of an old newspaper obituary reporting the death of Dr. Thomas M. Schad, Jr. at fifty-eight years of age in 1950. The accompanying black and white photo of him showed an older white man wearing a vintage pinstripe suit. His hair was white, and he had a matching thick beard. The article itself was very short, mentioning only that he was a pediatrician, a widower, and had a daughter named Catherine who'd died a few months after she was born.

"This doesn't mean anything," Jim said as they leafed through the additional papers in the folder, which were a mix of medical and personal information. "You could have just picked some random guy out of an old newspaper to show us."

"And if you physically met with him, he obviously wasn't dead," Sarah said. "We're not fools."

Beth shook her head and pointed at the folder. "No, that's him. I swear that's the man I met with."

"Mr. and Mrs. Knox, we don't gain anything by making up such an outrageous claim," the judge said. "And I've brought proof." He reached back into his briefcase and pulled out a business card in a plastic bag. "The good doctor left his fingerprints on this when he spoke to my daughter." He handed the bag to Jim. Through the plastic Jim could see the card had fingerprint ink on the front and back, revealing a perfect forefinger and thumbprint. The front of the card read:

Dr. Thomas Schad

(888) 667-3981

"I had it matched against the surviving FBI records they had for the Schad family," he continued. "The FBI had been keeping an eye on the family for a number of years. Apparently his father was some sort of crackpot shrink."

Sarah snatched the plastic bag from Jim and dialed the phone on the table. The three of them watched in silence as Sarah's face puckered when she hung up the phone.

"What happened?" Jim asked.

"It's disconnected," she said and threw the baggie back on the table. Jim tapped the side of his head with his left hand and sat back down, placing the folder back on the table as well. He glanced over at Beth, who stroked Michele's forehead.

"It's been out of service ever since that night," the judge said, corralling the folder and card and putting them both back in the briefcase. "And I can't track down any record of that number ever being issued."

"I know how all this must sound, but it's true," Beth said, lifting her head. "I swear that's the man I met that night."

"And you've been so truthful with the world up until now," Sarah said.

"You're right. You have no reason to believe anything we say," the judge said as he put his finger on the table while still staring at Sarah. "But I want you both to understand something, Mrs. Knox," the judge said. "Whether you believe us or not, Calvin isn't going to jail for either the deal he made with Dr. Schad or the assault charges from today. In fact, I've already cleaned up the little incident across the street, so neither Calvin nor your large Asian friend will be arrested for anything."

"How could you do that?" she asked.

"I did it to help your friend. Cal would have hung him out to dry if I didn't do what I did. You saw what the police were already thinking."

"But Cal can still be prosecuted if Dr. Dead Guy's video comes out," Jim said.

"No, he can't," the judge said. "There's no evidence that other child in the video ever existed. None. Dr. Schad took care of everything for Cal and Beth. And you can't prove what you just saw in a court of law because no one can recreate what happened."

"You're a liar," Sarah said. "You're both liars, and I don't buy it. He mentions Jane on the video I shot. Between that video and this one coming out, I'll make sure people put two and two together."

"Jane?" Beth asked, her face turning pale. "She already had a name?"

"Yes, her name was Jane Scanlon, and you killed her."

Beth said, "The doctor never told me her name. Neither did Cal."

"And you're wrong, Mrs. Knox," the judge added. "Cal's legal team could shred that video apart just by attacking your motives for releasing it. And without Jane's body to match against the doctor's video, Cal will never see the inside of a jail cell. But there will be rumors and scandal, and it'll be on every news channel for months. But no one involved will go to prison. Ever."

"It won't bring back Jane, either. I wish it would."

"We're not covering up your crimes!" Sarah said. She folded her arms and leaned over to where her husband was sitting. "Jimmy, give me the phone. I'm posting that video online right now."

"If you do that, it will destroy everything good that has happened since that time," Beth said. "Michele's story raised millions of dollars, not just for SMA, but for hundreds of charities. If that video is released, it's all for nothing. The funding and goodwill is all going to disappear."

"All you'll really have is your revenge against Cal, and millions will suffer because of it," the judge said.

"Mr. Knox, Jim," Beth said and nodded towards the door. "You were upstairs earlier. You saw what those parents are going through, didn't you?"

"I did, but that doesn't mean—"

"Do you two have kids?" Beth asked him.

"No, we don't."

"Then try to imagine having unconditional love for someone, and that you're partially responsible for their suffering. SMA is a genetic disorder. Both parents have to carry this genetic mutation for your child to develop the disease."

"But you didn't mean to give Michele the disease," Jim said. "You can't blame yourself."

Sarah swallowed, looked at the floor and kept her arms folded.

"It's hard telling yourself that as you're forced to feed your baby girl through a syringe. Or as you're sitting there watching the physical therapist use elastic bands to move your baby's arms. My baby girl had a stranger moving her like a puppet. It was awful to watch."

The judge said, "There's a bill in Congress right now that would provide billions of dollars of funding and research grants for this disease and dozens of genetic disorders. It's expected to pass by the end of the month. It could literally save hundreds of thousands and possibly millions of lives."

Sarah paced back and forth behind Jim while they spoke. "Two wrongs don't make a right!" She turned to her husband. "You can't listen to any of this. Give me the phone, Jimmy. Please."

"Why haven't you just had the police take the phone?" Jim asked them.

"That was my plan," the judge said. "But Beth made me promise I would let you two make the decision, and you don't break a promise to someone you love."

Beth made another appeal to both of them. "I had a choice to make that night. A choice that I wouldn't wish upon anyone. Jim, Sarah, I'm not asking you to believe me. What I'm asking you to do is show mercy and compassion not only for the people involved, but for those kids. They don't deserve to suffer with this disease anymore. Please."

Sarah pulled at his shirt sleeve and nodded towards the door. "Let's go, Jimmy. My husband and I aren't interested in helping—"

He got out of his chair and looked at the Snyders. "I want some time to discuss this with my wife. Alone."

The Judge looked at his watch. "It's one now. I've informed the police Calvin's presence is needed for his trial, so he's been taken by federal marshals down to the courthouse. I can keep him there until around six. At that point, he'll be free to go, so figure out if you only want to do what's best for you, or if you want to do what's best for everyone."

"You arrogant son of a bitch," Sarah said. "We didn't—"

"We're going," Jim said, taking his wife's hand. "But we can't make any promises either way. Because I still can't wrap my head around what a dead guy needs this money for."

"It's not going to him directly," Beth said. "It was in the contract that the payment be a large, anonymous donation made in his memory to the Ronald McDonald House charities."

Sarah just shook her head and laughed. "Unbelievable."

"What's so funny?" the judge snapped.

"If we do what you want, Cal's the one making this donation, right?"

"Yes, that's correct."

She looked at them with obvious disdain. "Cal will get a tax break for it." Sarah pulled her hand away from Jim's and stormed out of the room, slamming the door behind her. Michele's eyes popped open at the sound of the door. She whimpered and fussed for a moment before settling back into her mother's arms.

"I'll call you at six if you don't call me at the courthouse before then," the judge said and handed Jim his business card. "Here's the number."

Jim took the card from him. "We'll be in touch."

"Goodbye Jim," Beth said as he opened the door, "I'm sure you'll do the right thing."

15

It was 1:15 by the time Jim had chased Sarah back to the parking lot. She rattled the van's windows as she slammed the door behind her. He got in the driver's side and looked at her.

"I guess you don't want to talk about what just happened?" he asked.

"Drive," she said.

Checking his pants pocket to make sure the phone was there, he closed the door and pulled his seatbelt on. He started the car and turned onto Spruce Street away from the hospital. They rode for fifteen minutes in total silence, and Jim wondered what in the world he was supposed to do. "You have to admit, it's pretty weird all—"

"I don't have to admit anything," she snapped. "When we get home, I'm going make sure that video is everywhere. They made their decisions, and they have to deal with the consequences."

"I know," he said. "But when we get there, let's just take some time to talk this through."

"I don't need time," she said through clenched teeth. "You don't reward people like that."

"Sarah, sweetie, those kids—"

"Don't you dare," she said, shaking her head. "What if they were selling cocaine but giving all the money to charity? Or running a prostitution ring? Everything's fine by you as long as the money goes to charity?"

"No, that's not what I'm saying. I just think in this case . . ." He bit his lip and thought for a few minutes about what she said. He snapped his fingers and pushed a button on the hands-free unit.

"Call Token," he said. The unit dialed and rang Eric's number. She asked, "What the hell are you doing?"

"I just want to—"

"Eric Dawkins," the phone answered.

"Eric, it's Jim," he said.

"What's the matter, Cheat—"

"Dude, not now, okay?" Jim asked.

"Alright, alright. What's up?"

"What's your opinion about that case against Cal Nolan in court right now?"

"It's a joke."

"Really?" Jim's eyebrows went up. Sarah didn't move in her seat.

"Absolutely, a total bullshit case."

"Why?"

"The plaintiffs are trying to argue Nolan used age discrimination and sexual discrimination, except Nolan fired everyone. He didn't discriminate. I'm impressed the plaintiffs lawyers even got it this far."

"So when do you think it'll be wrapped up?"

"Normally I'd say in a couple years, but rumor has it the plaintiffs are drowning in fees. They must have been hoping for a quick settlement, which hasn't happened, so who knows."

"But if it's bullshit, why do they still think they'll get him to settle?"

"Well, if they can get it to the discovery phase, the plaintiffs lawyers will get to dig around and maybe they'll find some type of dirt on him. I think they're grasping at straws, but who knows, they might get lucky."

"What kind of dirt?" Sarah asked.

"Oh hey Sarah, didn't know you were there. Um, well, I'm sure they're hoping to find something in his financial statements that might implicate him in something sleazy. I'm guessing since Nolan's got that post-nup, they'd be looking real close for something about an affair and then try and blackmail him. Not exactly how they teach you to do it in law school, but it happens in these cases."

"So how much would it cost Nolan to settle?" Jim asked.

"I dunno, couple million dollars."

"And how much is he looking at in legal fees if it goes to the discovery phase?"

"Couple million dollars."

"Are you serious?"

"The guy just wants to win, that's all."

Jim closed his eyes and nodded. "Thanks," he said. "That was very helpful."

Sarah hung up the call. "Thanks for that, but I already know Cal's sleeping around."

"I know but think about it for a minute," Jim said. "The judge is dismissing a bullshit case where the plaintiffs' lawyers are just looking for dirt."

"It doesn't make him any less crooked."

"You can at least understand where the judge is coming from, can't you?"

Sarah pulled the ponytail out of her hair and shook her head. "No, I can't. He doesn't get to follow the law only when it's convenient for him and neither does Beth."

"She has Michele dying in front of her with this horrible disease, and she can save her. You don't at least consider that, especially if she thinks Cal is going to kill Jane anyway?"

"So now you actually believe that Cal threatened that?"

"I don't know," he said, watching the road in front of him. The van zipped along the interstate past the exit before Springfield. He looked at her and shrugged. "I didn't when she first said it, but after seeing your video and now hearing what Eric said, it seems like he'd do anything to be with Karen. I know I'd do anything to be with you."

"What are you saying?" she asked. "You'd kill a child to be with me?"

He put his hand on her leg. "No, I'm not saying that. I just think it's at least plausible that Cal might have, that's all."

She threw his hand back on his side of the car. "I don't like where you're headed with this. There is no way we're letting them get away with everything they've done."

"Did I say that?" he asked, gripping the steering wheel with both hands. "But I don't think we should make a snap decision with this much riding on what we decide."

She turned in her seat and talked over the police sirens that wailed past them. "That woman just told you she let a dead man save her baby by killing Jane. And now she claims the only way to save all these dying children is to cover up a conspiracy with the man who physically and verbally abused your wife for days, and you're taking her seriously?"

Jim looked over at her and squinted. "You think I don't know what happened to you? You think I don't want to see Cal pay for putting his hands on my wife?"

"I don't know, you tell me."

He slammed his hand on the steering wheel. "That's not fair! I want to see Cal get what's coming to him, but you heard the judge. They're not going to jail. And since that's the case, what does this accomplish?"

"Jimmy, they're both lying," she said, raising her voice. "They want to protect themselves and said whatever they had to say."

"So they just threw in the whole dead guy thing to add credibility?" he asked and accelerated through traffic to get to their exit. "Maybe they are little crazy, but wouldn't you be if your kid had somehow been pulled from the brink of death by a stranger?"

"No, because I would never make a deal like that!"

"You don't know what you'd do until you're in that situation."

"I'd like to think I'd always make the right decision. Just as I always assumed you would."

He shook his head and took a deep breath, exhaling and looking at the line of cars waiting to turn onto their street. "And what do we tell the Feeleys after this whole thing comes out?" he asked.

"You tell them you did what you thought was right."

He threw up his hands as they sat waiting to turn. After a minute or so passed, the light changed and they entered their development. "How? How exactly do I do that? I saw them sitting in that room, listening to the case worker tell them how their son is slowly going to waste away as his short life is spent using machines to do anything. Were you even listening to me as we walked out to the van after I saw that kid?"

"Yes, of course I was listening to you," she said. "That disease is cruel and awful, and no child deserves to suffer like that. But the end doesn't justify the means, and just because Beth is trying to fight this disease now, doesn't mean that excuses what any of them did."

"Sarah, you admitted the only thing we can prove is Cal was having an affair with that video. And you were right before, that's not illegal and should only be between a husband and wife."

"That was before he assaulted me! That was before he humiliated me!" she yelled. She took a deep breath and stared at him. "I can't believe this. I can't believe my husband would ever consider helping people cover-up a crime."

"You know, when I was president—"

"A Ford joke? A fucking Ford joke?" she said and tried to grab the phone from his pocket. "Give me that you asshole!"

"Stop, I'm sorry. I'm sorry," he said, as he fended her off. "I was just trying—"

"Don't sorry me. This isn't a gag. And if you delete that video—"

"I know it's not a joke. Just back off and let me think, okay?" he asked, pulling in their driveway and parking the van. Jim scratched his chin and looked at her. She folded her arms and looked away from him. The passenger cabin was silent for a minute while he thought about what to do.

He unbuckled his seat belt and faced her before he proceeded. "Alright, Sarah. I'll make you a deal. If you still feel this way at six tonight, we'll do it your way."

Sarah looked at him. "You really mean that?"

"I do," he said, nodding at her. "I'm not going to pretend I'm comfortable with this, but I trust your judgment. So if you still feel this strongly about it in a few hours, I'll support you."

"I don't need a few hours, Jimmy. I know what the right thing to do is right now," she said as she undid her seatbelt and edged towards him.

"Nevertheless, I'm going to hold onto the phone until six. I just want to make sure that's what you decide after we've given it some time."

"But Jim I—"

"Sarah, I was ready to move to Texas yesterday at noon. Now I'm working full time at CRC. And all kidding aside, what I was trying to say earlier about President Ford was everyone thought that pardon he gave was an awful idea when he did it. Then twenty-seven years later he's standing onstage at the JFK Library getting an award for it. Sometimes, a little time can help make things clearer. Don't you agree?"

"Okay, I'll wait. But I'm not planning to change my mind about this."

I know, he thought. They opened their respective doors and climbed out of the van. Sarah headed towards the house as he walked down to check their mailbox along the street. As he reached the end of the driveway, he heard Sarah's voice coming from the front steps.

"Reggie, get back here!" she yelled. He watched their new cat scurrying away from her, apparently having escaped when she opened the front door. Sarah started down the steps to go after the kitten, but Jim put his hand up to stop her.

"Stay there, I'll get him," he said, jogging after the cat onto their small front lawn. The cat ran away from his futile attempts to catch it and headed towards the sidewalk.

"Man, you're quick," he said as he trotted back towards their mailbox along the road, where the cat was curled up. "Now don't move." He leaned down to pick up the purring kitten.

"Hi Mr. Knox!" Marianne yelled from her front step and came charging towards him. The cat became spooked and darted into the street.

"I'll get him!" Marianne said and ran into the road to catch Reggie. Jim ran towards her as a car crested the hill. He saw the driver fiddling with her cell phone through the front windshield. Marianne screamed as Jim pushed her out the way.

The car's brakes squealed, but it was too late. The impact threw Jim backwards several feet. He hit the sidewalk and heard Sarah scream just before he lost consciousness.

16

The last few hours had been a blur for Sarah as she sat by herself in the chapel of Polk Memorial Hospital a few miles from their house. She'd never seen anyone bleed like Jim had as she'd cradled his head in her lap and waited for the ambulance to arrive. Carol and Marianne had followed in their car, and Sarah had left several teary messages for his family and hers as Jim was rushed into surgery. He was still breathing as they'd brought him in, but she'd heard the ER doctor on call say Jim's eyes weren't responding when she'd been ushered out of the triage area.

She looked up at the cross in the front of the empty chapel and bent down to pull out the kneeler. She crossed herself before bowing her head to pray.

Please God. Please help my Jimmy.

She heard a voice from the back of the chapel. "Mrs. Knox?"

Sarah looked back, and Dr. Kauffman, one of the ER doctors she'd met earlier, came towards Sarah in her blood-soaked scrubs. Sarah could tell from the doctor's pained expression it wasn't good news. "Yes, Dr. Kauffman. How is he?"

"There's no easy way to tell you this, Mrs. Knox, but your husband is brain dead," Dr. Kauffman said. "We'll do another scan in a few hours to fulfill the legal—"

"No, you're wrong," Sarah said, shaking her head. "You're wrong. You have to be."

"I'm sorry, Mrs. Knox. We've tried everything."

Sarah grabbed her purse and rifled through it. "But Jimmy has such a hard head. Once he asked if I wanted some walnuts and I told him we didn't have a nutcracker and then he said he had one called Sarah and I didn't think that was funny so I went to leave and he tried to crack a walnut on his head to make me laugh and I did so he tried to crack all of them that way. Dammit!" She threw her purse down when she couldn't locate any tissues and buried her head in her hands.

The doctor gathered Sarah's purse for her. "Your husband sounds very sweet. And he did a very brave thing to save that little girl's life."

Sarah took the purse from the doctor. "He's Jimmy."

"Why don't you let me take you upstairs to his room?" Dr. Kauffman asked. "I'll make sure you can spend some time alone with him for the next few hours."

"Thank you," she said. "I'd like that very much."

Sarah headed out of the chapel and back towards the waiting room where Marianne slept on Carol's lap. Carol's face looked haggard.

Sarah shook her head.

"I'm so sorry, Sarah," Carol said, but Sarah waved her off.

"It's not your fault, Carol," Sarah said, but she didn't stop following the doctor. When Sarah entered Jim's room, she saw he was surrounded by machines and had a tube down his throat. A clock above the door read 5:30 p.m.

As the doctor departed, Sarah set her purse down on the small table by the door, walked to the bed and pulled a chair up next to

Jim. A blue tray on the bedside table contained his personal effects, including his keys, wallet, and the new phone he'd bought that was barely scratched from the accident. She took his hand between hers and pulled it to her face, rubbing and kissing it as she locked her fingers around his and looked at him.

"I am so sorry, baby," she said. "I should have just let Cal have that stupid cupcake." The ventilator wheezed and Jim's EKG monitor beeped as she took one hand and stroked his face, making sure she didn't disturb the breathing tube.

"I'm going to miss you so much, Jimmy. The last time I didn't have you in bed with me at night was almost four years ago. Do you remember that?" She smiled as the memory of the day came back to her. "You had a business trip in Miami, and I asked you if you had everything packed from the list I made, and you said yes except for me. I thought that was so sweet until you asked me if I wanted to come and groped me from behind as I was making breakfast," she said, laughing and crying at the same time. "You make me so happy, sweetheart." Sarah leaned over and whispered in his ear, "And you'll be a great dad, Mr. President."

There was a knock behind her, and she turned to see the door pushed ajar by an older white man.

"Is this Jim Knox's room?" he asked.

"It is, but I was hoping—"

"Thank god. I've had a devil of a time finding this place," he said. He pushed open the door, put a laptop bag on the table next to her purse, and removed his hat to reveal his white hair, which matched his thick beard and moustache. He adjusted his glasses and walked over to her, pulling a penlight out of his black pinstripe suit pocket.

"Let's have a look here, shall we?" he asked and leaned over Jim, lifting up both eyelids and dancing the light around in his pupils.

"Have we met?" she asked. The man stopped and looked at her.

"My name is Dr. Thomas Schad and—"

Sarah slowly rose from her chair and stepped back from him. "You! That's how I know you. They said you were dead."

"What?" he asked, furrowing his brow. "Who told you I was dead?"

"Beth Groves and her father."

"I see," he said and continued his examination. "Tell me, Mrs. Knox, did they strike you as people who'd be averse to telling a lie if it helped their own interests?"

"No, they didn't. But they showed us this proof they—"

He clicked off the penlight and slipped it back in his pocket. "And this proof was more compelling than me standing here in front of you?"

"I suppose not," she said but backed up against Jim's bed rail.

"Please, by all means, you can see for yourself." The doctor extended his left arm towards her, and she grabbed hold of his sleeve and arm. "Satisfied?" he asked. She nodded and took her hand back.

"Good. I'm glad that silliness is behind us." Dr. Schad walked back to the table, sat down and set his laptop bag on the table. "Now, would you mind if—"

"I don't want to talk to you," she said, sitting back down by Jim's bed and stroking his face. "Just get out of here before I call the police."

"The police? Why on earth would you do that?"

"Because I saw what Beth let you do to that baby on that video," she said, looking back at the doctor. "All of you disgust me."

Dr. Schad pursed his lips as she spoke. "I must say, I'm a little surprised she felt so comfortable showing that procedure to a complete stranger. If you don't mind me asking, what else did she happen to mention?"

"I do mind. I don't care if Cal threatened to kill his baby or not, she—"

"Stop right there. Beth told you Mr. Nolan threatened to kill his child?"

"I don't believe anything those liars have to say at this point, but it doesn't matter to Jane now either way, does it? You all deserve to burn for this. So for the last time, leave me and my husband—"

"But Mrs. Knox," he said. "I can save your husband's life."

She turned away and focused her attention back on Jim, rubbing his hand. "I'm not a killer."

Dr. Schad stood up and walked over to Jim's bedside with his bag. "What if I told you no one else was needed in your husband's situation?"

Sarah turned her head towards him. "What do you mean?"

He removed his glasses and polished them. "It's a fairly simple procedure to cure your husband's condition. Just a few injections of a chemical compound I've developed, and he'll be on his way."

"I've never heard of a drug like this. And why wouldn't the hospital just give it to him if this cure was available?" she asked, looking at the numerous machines surrounding her husband.

"Oh, there's a number of factors which make it prohibitive for them, I suppose. Insurance regulations, FDA approvals, lack of funding for clinical trials, that sort of thing. But I assure you it will work. I don't get paid if it doesn't."

She swallowed hard and put Jim's hand against her face. "You mean it? No one has to die to save Jimmy?"

"Of course, I mean it," he said and pulled up a chair to sit down next to her. "When you go to see your doctor, he doesn't treat a broken leg the same way he'd treat a sore throat now, does he?"

"No, she doesn't."

"Exactly. Your husband is suffering from a much different ailment than Michele's and is therefore treated differently. So, does this mean you'd be interested in my services then?"

"I would if it meant—"

Dr. Schad grinned as he heard this. "Of course you would, Sarah," he said. "So let's get down to business." He took a clipboard from his bag and handed it to Sarah as he moved his chair closer to her.

"I have the agreement here, Mrs. Knox, but I'll need your signature on this HIPAA release form first," he explained and set a gold pen on the top sheet of paper. She picked up the pen and read it top to bottom before signing. He grinned as he took it from her, unclipping the sheet and folding it in two. He slipped it into his jacket before he continued. "There is the small matter of my fee. I work on a sliding scale, and the price varies depending on the patient's circumstances."

"And what price will I have to pay?" she asked as she reclaimed Jim's hand.

"A very small one, actually," he said and pointed at Jim's bedside table. "I can accept that phone as payment, if you stipulate that you'll forgive the parties involved and won't be pursuing this incident any further."

She grimaced and shook her head. "I knew it. Cal Nolan called you, didn't he?"

"I didn't say anyone called me. Perhaps I'm just not interested in haggling with the producers of *Inside Edition* to make sure my fee from the last job is collected."

"They aren't even sorry for what they did. There has to be another payment you'll take. Anything else."

"Mrs. Knox, I'd like to accommodate you," he said, sighing and turning his palms up. "I really would. But I need to put this matter to bed once and for all. I've got a number of patients I'm treating, and I can't have this one case monopolizing my entire practice. So this is the only trade I'm willing to accept."

She tapped her thumbnail against her teeth for a few seconds. He shrugged and picked up the clipboard. "But if you're not interested, I'm happy to—"

"Wait!" She slapped her hand down on the clipboard and pinned it back to the chair.

"Is something the matter, Mrs. Knox?"

Sarah closed her eyes and shook her head. "Don't go. I'll give you what you want. I don't care. I just want my Jimmy."

He crossed his legs and put his hands on his lap. "I don't know, Mrs. Knox. Your hesitation suggests you're not going to just let this matter drop even if you make this trade, and I'm not equipped to run around to make sure you've kept your word. I'm a doctor, not a policeman. I built my business on trust, and I'm not going to keep taking calls asking me to intervene because one party can't keep their word."

"I can move on. I'll do whatever I have to," she pleaded. "Just save Jimmy. Please."

Dr. Schad sat for a moment and folded his hands. "I'm sorry," he said and got out of his chair. "I don't believe you. Can you honestly say that if you give me that phone, that'll be the end of the matter and you'll just forgive the people who were involved?"

Sarah took a deep breath and didn't respond. He was right; she wouldn't be able to forgive them. She cursed under her breath and bent over in her chair, clutching her knees.

"That's what I thought." Dr. Schad took the papers from her.

She took Jim's hand and kissed it, fixing his wedding ring and smoothing his hospital gown. Dr. Schad packed his bag and rose from his chair.

"Please, Dr. Schad," she begged him. "I need Jimmy. He's everything to me."

"That's not my concern, Mrs. Knox," he said as he put on his hat. "But it does appear you two were great partners."

"We still . . ." She stopped speaking as she touched the bandage on Jim's head. "Wait!"

The doctor sighed and kept walking towards the door. "There's nothing more we have to—"

"I can just give them a pardon, right? I don't have to forgive them."

"A pardon?" he said, hesitating as he took hold of the door handle. "I don't understand what you mean."

"As long I let it go and don't pursue it any further, I don't technically have to forgive them, do I?" she asked, walking towards the doctor with the phone. "I just have to pardon them."

"Well I suppose, Mrs. Knox, but I just can't believe you suddenly—"

"Dr. Schad, please. Don't punish Jim because I took that extra second. I might struggle with forgiveness, but if I lose Jimmy, I'll never let this go, and my life will be dedicated to bringing all of you down. And I don't take losing well. I promise you."

He removed his hand from the door and turned towards her. "So you'd be willing to grant them this pardon, as you call it, even though you don't technically forgive them?"

"That's right. If it means I get the man I love."

"But you said earlier we should all burn for what we did. I find it hard to believe that you'll—"

Sarah moved closer and cradled the phone in her hand. "This isn't a blanket pardon, it's just a 'Get out of Jail' free card. So once we've made our deal, the card will be gone. But I'd suggest you don't try starting another game with me, because the next time you land in jail, you'll have to pay." Sarah held the phone out in Dr. Schad's direction and locked eyes with him.

Dr. Schad took off his glasses, looking at her and then towards Jim. He chewed on the ear piece, then placed the glasses back on his face and set his laptop bag on the ground. Reaching down and taking out the clipboard he'd given her earlier, he said, "This agreement cannot be changed, altered, or re-structured for any reason. You either accept all the terms and conditions or you don't. Do you understand?"

"I understand."

Dr. Schad handed her the documents and reached back in his coat pocket to pull out his gold pen. "Very well, Sarah," he said. "Please sign where you see the X." He handed her the pen, gesturing for her to sit down and sign at the table.

Sarah signed the paper and left the phone and clipboard on the table as she retook her position at Jim's side.

Dr. Schad walked over to Jim's bedside with his bag. He pulled out a small leather case with three syringes in it, each the same size and shape and filled with reddish-yellow liquid. He took rubbing alcohol and a cotton ball from his bag and cleaned an area on Jim's foot. Tossing the cotton into the trash, he gave Jim the three injections and slid the empty syringes back into the case one by one.

"It'll be a few moments before this takes effect," he said. Dr. Schad picked up the paper and phone off of the table and confirmed everything was in place on the written agreement. "So I'll say my farewell now before the celebration begins."

"Thank you, doctor," she said.

"Goodbye, Mrs. Knox. I will say, in all my years of practice, I've never met someone who begged for her husband's life while also threatening mine. Regardless, I won't be stopping my work with children anytime soon as long there are people willing to pay me."

"I warned you, doctor. I won't let you get away with this again. Why would you even bother when you don't keep the money?"

"Because," he said as he opened the door. "I wanted to do to something to honor my son's memory."

"Your son? The obituary said you had a daughter."

"I didn't have a daughter," he said. "But my son did."

Sarah's eyes widened and she whipped around.

"I told you, Sarah, the Judge and his daughter weren't averse to telling a lie to protect their secret. Michele's treatment was nothing compared to the procedure I administer to myself every day. But as they say, three shots a day keeps the reaper away."

"You're crazy," she said. "And I will find you, whoever the hell you are."

"Please, Mrs. Knox. Your warning is as meaningless as the one hanging in that crummy tiled office. But if you want to try Sarah," Dr. Schad smiled and tipped his hat at her as Jim's thumb twitched in her hand, "go ahead."

Author Christopher Finlan graduated from Temple University with a Bachelor's degree in history and has worked for the past six years in the software industry in the Philadelphia area. In his spare time, Christopher enjoys shopping for haircare products and driving his editor nuts with bad sentence structure. He resides in Wayne, PA with his wife Bridget and their two young children, Caitlin and Matthew.

Hillary Dunlop Schmid Hillary Dunlop Schmid graduated from Pennsylvania State University with a Bachelor's degree in Special Education and earned her Master's degree in Elementary Education at Rosemont College. She taught for eleven years in special education working with children with Autism, and is an advocate for children with Spinal Muscular Atrophy (SMA). Hillary is mother to twin sisters, Avery and Zane and wife to Keith. Since the loss of her daughter Zane, Hillary has made it her mission to raise awareness for SMA, and is a part of fundraising efforts to help find a cure for the disease. She resides in Malvern, PA.

TOGETHER
www.sweetbabyzane.com
FIGHT SMA

"The New Hollywood"

For more information about
The New Hollywood and its members,
visit their website at
www.TheNewHollywood.org

Interior and cover design and
complete book production provided by: